Straight From Nerdsville

Deena couldn't understand why she felt so bad after having her stupid little argument with Davey. But she did. She tried to just forget about it—and him. He was a jerk. A pest. A total nerd from Nerdsville. She really hadn't meant to be mean to him, but he'd pushed her into saying things that had hurt his feelings. Was that her fault?

Cranberry Cousins
BABYSITTER BLUES

BY CHRISTIE WELLS

A Troll Book

Library of Congress Cataloging-in-Publication Data

Wells, Christie.
   Babysitter blues / by Christie Wells.
     p.   cm.—(The Cranberry cousins; #6)
   Summary: Fifteen-year-old Deena is faced with two problems during
summer vacation: keeping her reluctant cousin, Kathy, interested in
the playgroup they run at the family inn, and evading the attentions
of a new boy she considers a nerd.
   ISBN 0-8167-1506-8 (lib. bdg.)   ISBN 0-8167-1507-6 (pbk.)
   [1. Cousins—Fiction. 2. Play schools—Fiction. 3. Interpersonal
relations—Fiction.] I. Title. II. Series: Wells, Christie.
Cranberry cousins; #6.
PZ7.W4635Bab 1989
[Fic]—dc19   88-16948

A TROLL BOOK, published by Troll Associates
Mahwah, NJ 07430

Printed in the United States of America.
10 9 8 7 6 5 4 3 2 1

Chapter 1

"Can you speed it up over there?" Kathy Manelli fumed. "We're not going to Tahiti, you know. Just to the town beach."

It was ninety degrees ouside, but her cousin Deena Scott was moving like molasses in January. Carefully Deena lined up the items on her bed and began packing her tote bag. She held up a blue T-shirt and then a green one against her turquoise bathing suit.

Kathy groaned. "They both look great but it doesn't matter. You wear them *over* the bathing suit. They don't have to match."

"Maybe the blue one, then," Deena said.

Kathy turned up the volume on her cassette player and nudged her sunglasses up over her nose. They had leopard-print wraparound frames that definitely looked punk. With her shades on and her favorite tape blasting, she could almost pretend she wasn't wasting an entire afternoon waiting for Deena to find a beach towel that matched her bathing suit.

"We're missing out on those prime-time tanning rays," Kathy reminded her.

"Too much sun gives you wrinkles," her blond-haired cousin replied. She put a book in her tote bag, took it out, and then removed a towel, which she re-folded with slow, painstaking care. "Do you want to have crow's feet by the time you're sixteen?"

"Oh, don't mind me," Kathy replied airily. "It's just this silly quirk I have about going to the beach while it's still light outside."

"Very funny."

Deena zipped up her tote bag, and Kathy sat up. She was finally ready.

"Oh, wait," Deena said, "I forgot my sunglasses. I thought I left them on my dresser. But they're not here. . . . " She began hunting around her unbelievably neat side of the room for the sunglasses, and with a sigh of exasperation Kathy flopped down on her bed again.

"Listen, if you didn't want to go to the beach to-day, why didn't you just say so?" Kathy asked.

Deena shrugged. "It's not that I don't want to go . . . but we've been to the beach practically every day since school ended." She located her sunglasses and put them in her bag. "Just hanging out, eating junk food, meeting up with kids from school . . . aren't you getting a little bored?"

"Bored?" Kathy echoed. "You make it sound like we're being forced to watch reruns of health class movies." Getting up off the bed, she shook her head in amazement. "This is what summer is all about—hanging out, having fun. Getting mindless. Why else does a person *slave* over their school work from September to June?"

Now it was Deena's turn to look amazed. "When did *you* ever slave over a textbook?"

"Just because I'm not Miss Honor Roll, like someone in this room, doesn't mean I don't deserve to rest my brain cells," Kathy replied.

"Right—all three of them," Deena muttered to herself as they started downstairs.

Luckily, her cousin didn't hear her. It took almost nothing for them to get into a full-scale argument now that school was out. During the school year, they more or less went their separate ways, and each had her own very different group of friends. But classes had been over for a while, and the two girls had spent almost every minute of that time with each other. It was almost enough to make them wish school would start again.

But it seemed that they were stuck with each other for the summer. Deena's boyfriend, Ken, had left for a job as a camp counselor in Maine, and her best friend Pat had gone to Colorado to spend the summer on her uncle's ranch. Kathy's friend Ellecia was at a summer camp, and Kathy's boyfriend, Roy, was working as a handy man, doing odd jobs all over town.

Stuck with each other, Deena repeated in her mind. I'll never get through the summer without going crazy, she thought. Not if she didn't find something more interesting to do than hang out at the beach and watch Kathy change the tape in her cassette player every fifteen minutes.

But what could they do? They had wanted summer jobs, but they were both responsible for chores at the Cranberry Inn, where they lived with their mothers and Kathy's younger brother, Johnny. It was not quite a year since Deena's mother, Lydia, decided that she and her sister, Nancy, should move to Cranford to reopen the old inn that had been run by their grandparents. Deena and her mother had moved down from Boston, and Kathy and her mother and brother had moved all the way from San Francisco to the quaint New England village.

With a lot of hard work they had fixed up the rambling Victorian hotel and had the grand opening on Thanksgiving weekend. Since then the inn had been doing well. Their mothers expected business to be booming over the summer. There were already plenty of guests coming and going. Deena and Kathy had to pitch in and help out—even though it was work they didn't get paid for. Still, their responsibilities at the inn made it impossible to get the kinds of full-time jobs other kids were getting this summer.

Not that Kathy would be interested in giving up any of her precious hang-out time in order to do something constructive, Deena thought as she watched her cousin adjust her sunglasses in the foyer mirror.

Just then Kathy jumped aside as a little red-haired

4

boy waving a butterfly net ran through the foyer. "It's my turn now, Todd! You said I could. You promised."

A second boy, with blond hair, chased after him, shouting, "Give it back!" He came to a sliding halt in front of Kathy, and she realized that Brian with the butterfly net was hiding behind her. "Make him give it back," the blond-haired boy demanded.

"You said I could use it, Todd. It's not fair." Brian protested.

Kathy looked from one angry little face to the other. She wasn't used to being a referee for squabbling six-year-olds. Just because she was older than they didn't mean she could decide who should get to play with the butterfly net. "Uh—do you guys have a mother or father around here somewhere?" she asked.

"Let me see that net," Deena said, walking over to join in the fray. "Gee—it's gigantic. You could fit an elephant in here. Have you guys caught anything with this yet?"

"I caught a big orange butterfly this morning," Todd said.

"But we didn't have anything to put it in, so it got away," Brian added.

"Oh—too bad," Deena said sympathetically.

A few moments later Deena had settled the fight by persuading the boys to go butterfly hunting together. One would be in charge of the net, and the other in charge of a coffee can, which Deena had found in the pantry, that would hold the butterflies.

The two boys ran off happily together through a field behind the inn, and Deena and Kathy got on their bikes and started for the beach.

"Gosh, don't those kids have parents?" Kathy said.

"I guess when you're on vacation, it's hard to keep track of little kids," Deena replied, pedaling along beside her.

They rode along for a few minutes without talking. It wasn't the first time Deena had taken charge of mischievous little guests like Todd and Brian. Now that it was summer, there were many children at the inn. Their parents wanted to relax, and often let the children run around unsupervised, trusting they couldn't get into *too* much trouble. It was getting to the point, however, where the atmosphere at the inn was anything but relaxing.

What the inn really needed was someone to watch the kids for a few hours every day, Deena thought. Maybe get them involved in some activities. "Hey! Wait a second!" she said out loud.

Kathy slowed her bike and turned to look at her. "Don't tell me you forgot something and have to go back. I'll scream."

"I just got the greatest idea! We can do something that's fun this summer and earn lots of money, too."

"I like the fun part. And the money part sounds good, too." Kathy gave her cousin a skeptical glance. "But something tells me this brainstorm of yours is going to be an awful lot like work, Deena."

6

"Just listen," Deena said patiently. "Why don't we start a play group at the inn? Guests could drop off their kids for a few hours in the morning and go sightseeing or shopping. We'd have automatic customers. Not to mention folks in town who might want to do it, too."

"Automatic customers like Brian and Todd, you mean," Kathy said. "No, *thanks*. Figuring out which little monster gets to use the butterfly net is *not* my idea of a great time. A few hours of that and somebody will have to take *me* away in a net!"

"Oh, come on, Kathy. It will be fun. And we'd really be *doing* something meaningful. You know, Socrates said, 'To do is to be.' And Plato said, 'To be is to do,' " Deena quoted proudly.

"And what about 'Girls just want to have fun'?" Kathy asked in a serious tone. "From *my* favorite philosopher, Cyndi Lauper."

"Come on, Kathy," Deena persisted, ignoring her sarcasm. "Once they stopped fighting, those little guys were really cute. Admit it. You thought so, too."

"Wait a microsecond, here! Let's get something straight. My idea of a really cute guy is one who's at eye level and drives around on something without training wheels. You have some *truly* weird ideas about how to have fun, Deena," Kathy added in a concerned tone.

"Well, I don't think it's weird to want to earn some money over the summer. Besides, what are we doing now every morning? Making beds and running to get towels and ice cubes for people," Deena said, pedaling faster and forcing Kathy to keep up with her. Her cou-

7

sin was so stubborn sometimes. . . . *most* of the time. She wouldn't know a good idea if it bit her on the nose!

"You're right," Kathy agreed after a thoughtful moment. "Helping around the inn every morning is getting to be a drag. I think I'll start sleeping late."

"Oh! What's the use?" Deena asked, looking up at the clear blue summer sky. As she pushed her ten-speed into high gear Kathy's laughter rang out behind her.

Kathy was content to forget all about Deena's suggestion for starting a play group. But Deena wasn't. As they settled themselves on the beach, she thought of nothing else. Kathy put on tanning lotion, plugged into a tape of her favorite group, Nuclear Waste, and closed her eyes in blissful contentment. She didn't even notice that Deena was scribbling away on a pad beside her, figuring out all the details.

Deena looked at her cousin and frowned. If Kathy wouldn't help her, she would find someone else. Or maybe she'd do it herself. Who needed a prima donna like Kathy to help anyway? Most of the time she was as hard to deal with as any spoiled five-year-old.

* * *

That night at the dinner table Deena was lost in thought, trying to figure out just what was the best way to convince her mother and aunt to let her start a play group.

"Deena," Mrs. Scott said for the second time, "would you pass me the bread?"

Deena looked up in surprise and reached for the bread basket. "Sorry, Mom. I was just thinking about the kids staying at the inn."

"You were?" Kathy's mother, Nancy, looked amused. "That's exactly what we were just talking about."

Lydia frowned. "Did either of you see two small boys with a butterfly net today?"

"Did we ever!" Kathy said. "Actually, Deena got them out from underfoot. She sent them butterfly hunting."

"Well," Lydia continued dryly, "after they went butterfly hunting, they decided to play catch, which would have been fine except that they chose the main parlor as their ball field. And they broke that old china lamp. It wasn't a priceless antique," she continued with a sigh, "but it was your grandmother's favorite." She smiled at her sister. "Remember, Nancy? She used to do all her hand sewing by it."

"I remember." Nancy smiled at the memory. "I thought at first we might be able to glue it back together, but it really is smashed to bits. I guess these things are bound to happen."

Lydia stared into her teacup, frowning. "What I'd like to know is why those kids were playing ball in the house. They should have been playing outside."

"They *were* outside," Deena said. "I guess they got bored."

"Maybe we should fix up some type of game room for the children," Nancy suggested. "Something with a lot of padding, where our more unruly little guests could bounce off the walls?"

"I don't know," her sister replied thoughtfully. "We really don't have the space. Besides, they might get too rowdy."

"Not if someone was watching them, kind of supervising their play," Deena said.

Kathy groaned and put her chin in her hand. "Here we go again . . . the great Romper Room brainstorm," she muttered.

"I had the greatest idea today," Deena cut in, ignoring her cousin. "What if Kathy and I started a play group here at the inn? Parents could leave their children with us for a few hours in the morning, and we could keep them out of trouble. I think it would be really fun."

"That's a wonderful idea, honey," Lydia said. "But it's a big responsibility, and we can't afford to pay you. Maybe you can charge the guests a small fee. I do think you girls should get paid for the job."

Kathy's mother brushed back a strand of long brown hair. "Lydia's right. Running a play group is a big responsibility. It isn't easy to watch a group of young children." She glanced over at her daughter, who, at that moment, was very busy twirling her spoon in a bowl of half-melted ice cream.

"Are you sure you can handle a roomful of little kids, Kathy?" her mother asked pointblank. "You never were very interested in watching your little brother."

"That was different, Mom," Kathy said. "Johnny never listens to anything I say because I'm his sister."

For the first time since Deena had suggested it, Kathy gave some serious thought to the idea of running a play group. It was true that her first choice for a summer job would not have been amusing a bunch of kids. But maybe it wouldn't be so bad. Little kids could be fun. And although she would never admit it to Deena, Kathy was also getting a bit weary of dividing her day between chores at the inn and hanging out at the beach. It would only be a few hours in the morning. How hard could it be?

"All I'm trying to say is that caring for small children takes loads of patience, Kathy," her mother replied finally. "You have to keep your eye on them every single minute. You can't just space out."

"I wouldn't space out," Kathy insisted angrily. "And I have tons of patience!" Her mother gave her a skeptical look. "When I want," she added. "I'm practically a role model for little kids."

Kathy glared at her mother. Most of the time, Nancy Manelli was pretty cool—but sometimes, like right now, she treated Kathy like a kid. After all, nobody had given Deena the third degree about being patient and spacing out. It made Kathy furious—and determined to show everyone that she was just as patient and mature as her cousin Deena.

"A role model?" her mother teased. "Pardon me, I had no idea. Is this condition serious? Or contagious?"

Everyone at the table was laughing, and finally Kathy had to laugh too.

"O.K.," she said with a grin. "I'll admit it. I'm not exactly Mister Rogers. But I can get along with kids if I try. And I do want to earn some money this summer." She glanced over at Deena, knowing that her cousin was probably feeling quite pleased with herself by now. "A person has to think about more than just hanging out at the beach and eating junk food, you know," she added in a serious tone.

"Oh, really? Like what, for instance?" Deena asked suspiciously.

"Like . . . other things, Deena. Responsible stuff. You know what I mean." Kathy shot her cousin a look across the table that said, "Why are you arguing with me now that I'm finally agreeing with you?"

The truth was, Kathy had seen a great leather bomber jacket that would be perfect for school in the fall. If she saved her money from the play group, she could buy it. But her mother and Deena didn't need to know that.

Surprisingly, it was Deena's mother who was on her side. "Come on, Nancy. I think this will be a great experience for the girls. They'll be working with children and learning to run their own business, too." She turned to the girls. "You can fix up that storage shed behind the garage. It's not big, but it should make a decent playhouse. It will be nice to see you two tackling a big project like this together."

Deena stood up and gave her mother a hug.

"Thanks, Mom. The shed will be perfect. It just needs some paint. We can start working on it tomorrow!"

She glanced over at Kathy, who was busy stirring up her ice cream again, lost in her own thoughts. Deena just hoped that she and Kathy would be tackling the project . . . and not each other. If the past few months were any indication, the hardest part of this plan might be working together without strangling each other.

Though she could never tell what Kathy was thinking, she wondered if her cousin wasn't mulling over the same doubts. She couldn't help noticing that Kathy was showing that bowl of ice cream absolutely no mercy.

Chapter 2

"Yellow? Yuck! What a nerdy color." Kathy sat down on the grass and blew a strand of dark brown hair out of her eyes. "I suppose that next you'll be suggesting we paint little 'Have a Nice Day' happy faces all over the place."

"Scientific tests have proven that yellow is a cheerful, optimistic color, and that it puts children in a good mood," Deena said calmly. "And I don't want to paint happy faces on anything . . . but I *was* thinking of a smiling sun. Maybe a rainbow."

"This place is going to look like a big walk-in greeting card," Kathy said, glancing over at the small, weatherbeaten shed.

"Well, it's a whole lot better than your idea, Kathy. I hardly think that black and silver are appropriate colors for a playroom."

"O.K.—maybe that idea was a little much," Kathy

conceded. "Let's compromise. How about purple with silver stars? It would be bright and cheerful...in a spacy sort of way." From the stony expression on Deena's face, Kathy could tell her cousin hardly considered purple a halfway point between yellow and black.

"Purple is not a cheerful color," Deena said slowly, as if reaching the limits of her patience. "The kids are going to think they're on another planet. Their parents will think we're *from* another planet."

Sighing with frustration, Deena glanced down at her watch. It was already noon. She and Kathy had cleaned out the shed fairly quickly, but they were certainly wasting time hassling about what color to paint the four very small walls. Why couldn't they agree on anything?

"How's it going, girls?" Nancy asked. She had been weeding the garden, and was holding a handful of dandelions. She looked inside the shed. "It looks a lot bigger cleaned out. You ought to be able to get about a dozen kids in there. So what's next?"

"We're going to paint," Deena said.

"We're making it purple, with silver stars and planets," Kathy told her mother. "What do you think?"

"We're painting it yellow," Deena insisted, "with a smiling sun and a rainbow. That will be better for little kids, don't you think, Aunt Nancy?"

Kathy's mother looked at the girls and just laughed. "I think you ought to check the paint supply in the garage. As I recall, we only have a gallon or two of

16

plain, unexciting white left in there. Unless you girls plan on buying special paint?"

Deena and Kathy looked at each other. They both knew they didn't have any extra money for special paint. Their argument suddenly seemed rather silly and definitely a waste of time.

"I guess the outer space look is out," Kathy said, getting up from the grass.

"And the rainbow," Deena added with a sigh. "Well, let's get started."

"All right," Kathy agreed, following her toward the garage. "You know, Deena, maybe plain white won't be so bad. When the kids come, we can give them crayons and let them draw all over the walls. Wouldn't that look good?"

"It would look like the New York City subways!" Deena replied. "Let's just paint it. We can figure out how to brighten the place up later, O.K.?"

"O.K.," Kathy reluctantly agreed. She had a sneaking suspicion that Deena's idea of "brightening" would again include some nauseatingly cheerful decorator touch.

Deena found the paint while Kathy located the rollers and a pan. Kathy stared doubtfully at the spattered paint cans. "You sure you wouldn't consider tinting it?" she asked.

Deena shook her head. She hoped this play group scheme wouldn't turn out to be a total waste. It had seemed a good idea at first, but after barely a morning's work, she was starting to have her doubts.

It didn't take long for the girls to paint the inside of the shed. They had gotten plenty of painting practice that fall when they helped fix up the inn before its Thanksgiving weekend opening. But unlike the other times Kathy and Deena had painted together, this time they managed to get the job done without having a duel with wet paint.

Deena slid her roller off the wall with a flourish and stood back to survey their work. "This looks terrific," she said.

Kathy raised one eyebrow. "Well, it certainly looks white. Not exactly the most thrilling paint job I've ever seen, but I guess it will do." She wiped her hands on a rag and began collecting rollers and pans. "So I guess we're ready for the grand opening."

Deena shook her head. "There's still one little detail we have to work out."

"What's that?"

"How we're going to entertain a roomful of small children."

Kathy looked at her cousin in alarm.

"Don't worry," Deena said with a grin. "One of us was very organized this morning and went to the library and got out a few books on the subject. We can look at them while we eat lunch."

"I can't wait," Kathy muttered as they headed toward the house.

Deena paged through the activity books while Kathy made tuna fish sandwiches and ice-cream sodas. "Listen, it says that children love music and musical activities." Deena looked up at Kathy. "I guess we need some instruments."

"Good idea." Kathy thoughtfully nibbled on her sandwich. "I think Roy has an old guitar he doesn't use anymore. I'm sure he'll let us borrow it . . . but what will we do for an amplifier?"

"An electric guitar?" Deena rolled her eyes. "These kids are much too little for an electric guitar—with or *without* an amplifier. You have to start thinking more kid-size, Kathy. Didn't you play with little instruments when you were in nursery school and kindergarten? Little tambourines and shakers?"

"I don't remember tambourines and shakers," Kathy said, scratching her head. "But when I was that age, my dad used to let me stand on a chair and play his electric xylophone sometimes."

"His electric xylophone?" Deena took a deep breath and counted to five. It really wasn't Kathy's fault that she was so weird. She'd had an unusual upbringing, to say the least. Deena promised herself that she would try to have more patience with her cousin. "Listen, the point is, we need instruments for little kids. I think we can find a few things in the attic, and maybe we can make some."

After lunch, the girls set about assembling equipment for their play group. In the attic they found a long wooden whistle, a ukulele with two of the four strings missing, a pair of dusty bongo drums, a tambourine, and some New Year's Eve shakers.

Deena was satisfied with the collection, but Kathy

insisted on putting her big tape player in the room as well. She figured after all those tambourines and shakers, the kids would be ready for some real music—Nuclear Waste!

Pooling together a few dollars, the girls bought some crayons, construction paper, and finger paints at the variety store in town. Deena had some other art supplies at home, and Kathy pulled together a box of make-up and old clothes to play dress-up.

By early afternoon the girls were tired and hot. "I don't know about you, but I'm exhausted. What else is there to do?" Kathy said as she rubbed a spot of dirt on her knee.

"I guess we've done all we can for today," Deena said with a shrug as she surveyed the new playroom. Despite her earlier doubts, the room looked clean and bright and friendly. "See how much you can accomplish with a few hours of solid work?" she said. "Tomorrow we'll be ready for the kids."

"In that case I think I'd better prepare myself with a few solid hours of mindless hanging out at the beach," Kathy said.

Deena was suddenly nervous about the idea of actually starting their business tomorrow. "While we're sitting around, we can plan what we want to do with the kids tomorrow."

Kathy groaned. Deena would *never* understand the true meaning of mindless hanging out. If you wanted to get truly mindless, you weren't supposed to *do* anything. It was like a mystical, transcendental mind state, Kathy thought with a sigh. If a person didn't "get it," you just couldn't explain it to her.

*   *   *

At the town beach, the girls found a spot close to the water and stretched out on their towels. Following her usual routine, Kathy coated herself with suntan lotion, adjusted the straps on her purple bathing suit, and then plugged herself into her tape player. With her eyes closed, she lay back and gave out a contented sigh.

Off into the ozone in record time, Deena thought. She knew Kathy wouldn't return to earth again until she somehow sensed the approach of the Tastee-Freez vendor. It was uncanny the way she just popped up as soon as the guy came within twenty feet of the beach. Deena couldn't understand how Kathy did it. She certainly couldn't hear a thing above the noise on her tape player.

This meant, of course, that Kathy had no intention of discussing their plans for tomorrow's first play group session—at least not before the Tastee-Freez man showed up. Deena sighed and tossed down the pad and pencil she was holding.

I've worked hard all day, too, she thought. If Kathy thinks she can get out of planning part of this job, she's got a surprise coming. Maybe she thinks that by zoning out she can get me to do it all by myself. "Sorry, Sleeping Beauty," Deena told her slumbering cousin. "As soon as you wake up, we're having an organizational meeting here."

Deena got up and took a stroll down to the water to cool off. It was a hot day and the beach was packed.

21

She threaded her way through the crowds and waded knee-deep into the water. It felt icy against her hot skin. She stopped for a moment and watched the waves, trying to make herself jump in and get the agony over-with quickly.

Then, all of sudden, a body came hurtling through space and crashed into her. They both landed in the foamy surf face down. Deena pushed herself up, sputtering and coughing. She had sand in her mouth, her bathing suit . . . everywhere.

"Gosh—are you all right?" someone asked. "I'm really sorry . . ."

Deena blinked and pushed a wet glob of hair out of her eyes. A tall lanky boy with sandy-blond hair was staring at her with big, sorrowful eyes. He looks like a basset hound that knows he's in trouble, Deena thought.

"I'm O.K.," Deena said, wiggling away when he took her arm to help her up.

"Gosh—I could have killed you. You could have drowned or something," he said, sounding even more upset.

"I'm all right. Honest," Deena insisted as she straightened out her bathing suit. "It was just an accident. Don't get so hysterical." She wished he would go away and leave her alone. People were starting to stare at them.

"I was taking a really big wave on my boogie board," he explained. "I guess I sort of lost control."

"Sort of," Deena agreed snidely.

He might have been cute, she noticed, if he didn't have such a silly, toothy smile. And if his ears, which were sunburned pink on top, didn't stick out so much from his head. He had on big baggy jams that came down to his knees and were made of a wild-looking print material. Someone else might look really cool wearing a bathing suit like that, Deena thought. But not this guy.

He was still staring at her, that same unblinking basset-hound stare. It was really annoying, she thought, pushing back her hair with her hand.

"Uh—my name is Dave Findlay. Well, some kids call me Davey," he stammered nervously. "You could call me either, I guess."

"Thanks," Deena said, wanting to put a quick end to the conversation. She hoped she'd never see this nerdy guy again! She didn't care if he gave her permission to call him Pee-Wee Herman. "See you," she said, starting to walk back toward her towel.

"What's your name?" he asked, following her in spite of the fact that she was obviously doing her best to get away from him.

"What's the difference?" Deena said. She wasn't ordinarily rude, but she had a feeling that just breathing in this kid's direction would be misinterpreted as encouragement.

"Whenever I almost drown somebody, I like to know their name," he joked.

"If you're keeping a list, just mark me down as an unidentified falling object," Deena suggested.

Davey began laughing hysterically at her joke. "Unidentified falling object! Hey, that's really funny!"

Deena cringed. She tried to walk faster, but Davey's loping stride easily kept up with hers. He had a loud, hooting laugh, the kind that people always noticed. She was sure that any minute now she and this guy were going to run into someone from school, and she would absolutely die of embarrassment.

"What about your board?" she asked him suddenly, stopping dead in her tracks. "Don't you have to go find it? Someone might walk away with it."

"Nah—" He waved away her suggestion. "I know where it landed. No one will take it. I can pick it up any time."

"Oh," Deena said, starting to walk fast again. She didn't even look at him, hoping nobody would think they were together.

"But thanks for being so thoughtful," he added eagerly. "Especially after I knocked you down and all. You know, you never told me your name."

"I know," Deena said curtly. Finally her towel was in sight. Kathy was gone. Deena marched across the sand toward it, hoping she could get this boy to leave her alone before Kathy came back and started teasing her about him.

"Let me guess," he went on. "I'm really good at this. . . . You look like a Judy," he decided. "Or a Vicky maybe. Yeah—I think it's Vicky."

"Vicky?" He had finally gotten Deena's undivided

24

attention. "You think I look like a Vicky?" she demanded.

"I guessed it, right? I told you I was really good at this," he said with a smug look.

"No-o-o! You are absolutely and totally *wrong*." For reasons she could not explain, Deena could not imagine an insult worse than being told that she looked like a Vicky. "I despise the name Vicky!"

"Hey, Deena—want some Tastee-Freez?" Kathy asked, coming up alongside of her with a cup of the frosty concoction.

"Oh! It's Deena!" Davey slapped himself on the forehead. "I can't believe it. That was my next guess! Honest . . . "

Kathy suddenly noticed Deena's unwanted companion. She looked over at him, then at Deena with a smile on her face that said, "Where did you find this turkey?"

"Hi!" Dave said to Kathy. "My name is Dave Findlay. But some kids call me Davey."

"Hi," Kathy said, sitting down on her towel. "I'm Kathy, Deena's cousin."

"Hey, you guys are cousins? That's really neat."

Kathy laughed at his reaction. "What's so neat about it? It's not like we're Siamese twins or anything."

"Oh, I don't know." Dave shrugged and laughed. "I don't have any cousins . . . or sisters or brothers. So I guess I think it's neat to be able to hang out with someone who's related to you. Know what I mean?"

"Sure, I guess so," Kathy said, smiling at him.

Deena briskly dried herself with a towel. Why in the world does Kathy encourage this moron? she asked herself. Can't she see I'm trying to get rid of him?

"How old are you, Davey?" Deena suddenly asked him.

"Fifteen," he answered with a big grin. "Why?"

"Just asking," she replied with a shrug. For some reason she had thought he was younger, and that once he realized that, he'd be discouraged from trying to make friends with them.

"How old are you, Deena?" Davey asked.

"I'm almost sixteen," she said, knowing she was stretching it. Her birthday wasn't for months, but she had to make the most of whatever edge she might have over him.

"You're fifteen, too?" Uninvited, Davey sat down on the edge of Deena's towel. "Gee—you look really young for fifteen," he said, staring at her in amazement.

Deena felt her blood boiling. She could hear Kathy laughing softly to herself, and that made her even madder. First this guy had the nerve to tell her she looked like a Vicky, and now he was telling her she looked *young* for fifteen!

"That's funny," she said haughtily. "Most people think I look at least sixteen."

"Sixteen?" Davey shook his head. "No way. Gosh, back in Ames—Ames, Iowa, where I live—nobody would ever say you looked sixteen."

So, he was from Iowa—that figured. Deena had never met anyone quite as corny before!

"This is ridiculous," Deena muttered to herself. She simply refused to continue this dumb conversation with this knucklehead. "We've got to go, Dave. It's been ... interesting chatting with you." She jumped up abruptly and started packing her tote bag.

"Going home so soon?" Davey barely blinked as Deena gave her towel a powerful tug, pulling it right out from under him. Forced to sit on the bare sand, he stared up at her and smiled. "It's still early . . . "

"I've got things to do at home." Much better things to do than sit here and be pestered by you, she added silently. "Kathy . . . aren't you coming?"

"I think I'll just hang out for a while longer," Kathy said lazily, slipping her sunglasses down her nose to look at Deena. "Roy said he might get off work early today and meet me here."

"Oh—fine," Deena said, hefting the strap of her tote bag over one arm. "See you later."

"Hey, wait a second." Dave jumped up from the sand. "I'll walk you home, Deena."

Walk her home? Deena wanted to scream! Couldn't this guy take a hint?

"Uh—that's O.K., I'm probably not going in your direction," she said.

"Where do you live?"

"At the Cranberry Inn."

"Sure, I know where that is. I'm staying right near there, at my father's house."

27

"Oh—" Deena had hoped he was walking somewhere in the opposite direction—Iowa, for instance. "Well, I have my bike . . . "

"I have my bike, too," Dave said. "I'll just run and get my stuff and meet you at the bike rack—"

"But—" Before Deena could come up with another excuse, Dave ran off across the sand. When she got to the bike rack, she had an impulse to take off and leave without him. But something told her it wouldn't be worth the trouble. Davey would probably pedal extra fast and catch up to her in no time.

A few minutes later they were riding side by side along the road that led from the beach to town. Deena prayed that she would get back to the inn before any of her friends saw her with this guy.

She concentrated on pedaling and looking straight ahead. She didn't have anything to say to Davey and hoped that if she acted cool enough he would leave her alone in the future. For a while he didn't talk either, and she thought he was getting the hint. Then she realized he was probably just nervous.

"Hey—listen to this joke," he said suddenly. "Why can't you teach a chicken to play baseball?"

"I don't know," Deena replied in a bored tone. "Why?"

"Because they only hit *fowl* balls—get it?" he laughed.

Deena winced. Even Kathy's nine-year-old brother, Johnny, wouldn't tell such a lame joke. She

28

glanced over at him with a weak smile. "Yeah—I get it," she said.

Davey was quiet again for a while. Then he said, "I bet you get a lot of snow here in the winter. I bet it's really pretty here in the winter."

"Yes—it is," Deena replied, trying to get by on as few words as possible.

"I only come here in the summertime. My folks are divorced, and I live with my mother during the school year. I come here to visit my dad. I might live with him year-round . . . but I don't know yet. What's the school like here? Do you like it?"

He sure was a chatterbox, Deena thought. She was going to hear his whole life story whether she wanted to or not.

"The school is O.K. The kids are pretty nice. I've only lived here since last September. My folks are divorced, too. My mother and I used to live up in Boston, but we moved here when she decided to open the inn. That's when Kathy moved here, too," she added.

"It must be really neat to live in that old inn," Dave said, sounding wistful and envious.

"It's O.K." Deena replied.

"Must be lots of fun. A lot of people around all the time. Like living in a house with a really big family."

"Well, I guess so," Deena said. It was true. Living in the inn *was* like that sometimes.

"It's really a drag being an only child. I don't even have any cousins my age to hang out with. Oh, gee—I already told you that, didn't I?" he asked, sounding embarrassed.

"Yeah, you did, but that's O.K. I'm an only child, too, and I know what you mean," Deena said, trying to make him feel less self-conscious. Then she was mad at herself for being nice to him. Keep it up, Deena, and you'll never get rid of him.

"Well—here it is," Deena said with relief as the inn came into view. "Guess I'll see you around sometime."

"Are you coming to the beach tomorrow? We could ride down together."

"I don't know . . . I don't think so," Deena said, not wanting to hurt his feelings. Davey was looking at her with that forlorn expression again. Now that she knew more about him, she realized he was probably really lonely. But she still didn't want to be friends with him.

"I could stop by tomorrow afternoon on my way. Just to see if you're going . . ." he suggested, his voice trailing off on a hopeful note.

"No! I mean . . . no, thanks. I don't know what I'm doing tomorrow. I might not even be here," Deena said.

It wasn't *really* a lie. Even though she expected to be running their very first play group, anything could happen, she thought with a twinge of guilt. My mother could send me into town for something at the grocery store. I could get kidnapped by a band of gypsies . . .

"Oh—O.K.," Davey said reluctantly, getting back up on his bike. "See you, Deena."

"See you," Deena answered as she watched him

30

ride away. Finally he was gone! She would have to make sure she didn't run into him again. She'd be real careful at the beach, and if he came by the inn, she'd tell everyone to say she wasn't home. She was sure he'd give up pretty easily after hearing that a few times.

But somehow, as she walked her bike up to the garage, she had the oddest feeling that she had not seen the last of Dave Findlay.

Chapter 3

"So, what time is your new boyfriend picking you up today for the beach, Deena?"

"He's not!" Deena dug her spoon into a bowl of cereal and glared at her cousin across the table. "You're just being mean. You know I don't like that guy."

"Maybe . . . but he sure likes you. I bet he follows you around all summer."

Horrified by the very thought, Deena practically knocked her breakfast into her lap. "Don't even joke about a thing like that!" she snapped.

Kathy started laughing. "Well, sorry. But I bet he does. Guess that's the way guys are in his hometown. He doesn't exactly play it cool."

"He was just trying to be friendly, I guess," Deena said. What was getting into her? She was actually sticking up for someone she never wanted to see again? Or was she just feeling guilty about hurting his feelings?

"Come on, Deena," Kathy teased. "He wasn't that *friendly* to me. I think he's got a crush on you. I bet he asks you out."

"I'm *not* about to go out with that guy. I already have a boyfriend, remember?" Deena replied angrily. "I'm not even going to talk to Dave if I see him again. And if he comes here, everybody better say I'm not home. He'll get the hint."

"I doubt it," Kathy replied, spreading strawberry preserves on a slice of toast. "I don't know. I didn't think he was *so* awful. He was sort of cute . . . if you like that type."

"The goofy, totally nerdy type you mean?"

Kathy bit into her toast. "You said it, I didn't."

"Well, thanks for the insult," Deena said huffily.

"Look, I never said he was *your* type," Kathy added almost apologetically. "But you have to admit— he did think you were his . . . "

"Can we please talk about something else besides that pest Dave Findlay?" Deena begged her cousin. "We're starting the play group this morning, and we still don't even know what we're going to do with the kids."

When the guests had been informed that a play group was starting at the inn, five children had been signed up immediately. Deena wished that she and Kathy were starting with a smaller group their very first day, but there was nothing she could do about it now. She had tried to get Kathy to help her plan some activities for the children last night, but right after dinner Kathy had run off to practice with her band.

"Oh, don't worry about it," Kathy said airily, carrying her plate to the sink. "It's only three hours. We'll think of plenty of things to do. Let's just wing it."

As Deena's mother had predicted, their first morning running a play group proved to be a real learning experience for both Deena and Kathy. The lesson, Kathy decided much later, was never trust first impressions. As the morning began and Kathy and Deena introduced themselves to their new charges, Kathy was sure that the next three hours were going to be a breeze.

There were five children in all. Brian and Todd, the two six-year-olds who had been haggling over the butterfly net a few mornings ago, were the first to arrive. Compared to the other day, Kathy thought they looked very controllable. Brian had a three-year-old sister named Dara, who was clutching a ragged stuffed dog under one arm and sucking her thumb. Brian said she could talk, but she wouldn't say a word to either Deena or Kathy. A dark-haired girl named Kelly was also enrolled. She was just a little older than Dara and quite a chatterbox. She immediately latched on to Deena and began asking her a million and one questions, which Deena did her best to answer in a strained but very patient tone.

Charlie, seven years old and oldest of the group, was the last to arrive. When his father brought him down to the playhouse, they were both scowling. The girls guessed that Charlie didn't really want to be part of a play group—which he called that "bunch of little babies." However, he obviously had no choice. Sure she could win him over, Deena greeted him with a broad smile. Charlie responded by sticking his tongue out at her.

Deena decided they should start the morning off with a game of Simon Says. The kids seemed to like the idea and lined up, ready to play. All except Charlie, who sulked in the back of the room with his arms crossed over his chest.

"Come on, Charlie—don't you want to play?" Kathy asked him.

"No way! Simon Says is for babies. I don't play baby games like that."

Kathy was stumped for a reply. If the kid didn't want to play Simon Says, nobody was going to force him. Maybe once he saw the other kids playing, he would want to join in, she thought. "O.K. You can just watch then if you want," she said. "Maybe later we'll play a game you'll like."

"Yeah, right," Charlie grumbled.

The children quickly got bored imitating Deena as she energetically went through a "Simon Says do this . . . " routine.

"Can we go outside?" Brian asked.

"Let's go down to the pond and look for tad-poles!" Todd chimed in.

"Yeah—neat idea," Charlie said, suddenly losing his frown.

"Gee—I don't think we can go to the pond today," Deena said nervously as she pictured herself and Kathy fishing their precocious charges out of the muddy bog. "But why don't we go outside ... and, ummm ... " She shot Kathy a pleading look.

" ... and we can play hide-and-seek," Kathy suggested, naming the first game that came into her mind.

The children ran outside, except for Charlie, who dragged his heels and made a face. Kathy and Deena followed.

"So—how are we doing? It must be close to eleven o'clock already, I bet," Kathy said.

"Try nine-thirty," Deena said, checking her watch.

"Hide-and-seek should use up some time."

"Yeah—another five minutes at least," Deena agreed. "I didn't realize they got bored so quickly."

"They have a lot of energy. Let's try to tire them out," Kathy suggested.

Deena was right. Hide-and-seek didn't hold anyone's interest for very long. Kelly said she'd only hide if she could hide with Dara; Charlie refused to hide from "those babies," and Brian and Todd disappeared completely for a while. Kathy and Deena looked all over and couldn't find them. They started to get worried, thinking the boys might have run off by themselves into the woods, even though they had set strict limits on where the children could hide. Finally Kathy heard their muffled giggles and found them under the back porch.

"We need a new strategy," Deena decided.

"Right." Kathy gave a weary sigh. "How about food?"

The girls served juice and cookies, then decided to let the kids paint outside. At about a quarter to twelve Deena announced clean-up time. "Time to put everything away. Your parents will be here soon."

"Thank heavens . . . " Kathy mumbled under her breath as she tried to wipe yellow paint out of Kelly's hair. Todd had poked Kelly with a paint brush.

With her arms full of paint jars and paper, Deena led the group back to the playhouse. She barely noticed the thin stream of water on the path leading to the shed before she opened the playhouse door and a wave of water gushed through the doorway and washed over her ankles.

"What in the world . . . !"

The flock of children close behind her squealed and jumped back. Still clutching the supplies, Deena pushed the door all the way open and went inside. The little shed was flooded with about six inches of water. Deena looked down and saw a dress-up hat and a storybook float by.

"Kathy!" she screamed. "Get over here—and hurry!" She was about to yell that one of the pipes had broken when she realized that the shed had no plumbing.

Then Deena caught sight of a piece of garden hose. The hose had been cleverly slipped through the window and hidden behind a pile of books and cardboard cartons. She ran across the room, splashing through the water, and pushed the hose out the window.

"Oh, no!" Kathy appeared at the doorway looking shocked. "What happened! This place looks like it was hit by a hurricane."

"A hurricane named Charlie, I'll bet," Deena said. She slogged her way over to Kathy and sighed. "Well, let's give the kids back to their parents. Then I guess we'll have to clean up in here."

She didn't dare look at Kathy. She didn't have to. She knew her cousin had not counted on unexpected time-consuming disasters—like a full-fledged flood—the very first day. But this was a fluke. Things like this couldn't possibly happen every day. Even Kathy would have to admit that. Still, it was hard to tell which of them was more relieved when the parents finally collected their children.

They returned to the shed silently. Deena used a big broom to sweep out the remaining water. Kathy gathered up all the wet things and spread them out to dry on a hot sunny spot on the grass.

"Well, we sure cleaned up that mess quickly," Deena said brightly.

Her cheery voice was unusually irritating to Kathy, who was tired and cranky. "I don't know what you're sounding so chipper about," she grumbled.

Deena shrugged. "Well, it wasn't what we expected, but it was kind of fun."

"Yeah, great fun. I don't even feel like going to the beach today . . . since I did so much swimming in there."

39

"Kathy—come on. It wasn't that bad. It was our first day. We just need to keep a closer eye on Charlie. I'm sure he's the one who put the hose through the window."

"I wonder what he has in mind for tomorrow. Better have the fire department's phone number handy."

"Don't be so negative, Kathy. Let's give this a chance. You're just tired. It will go better tomorrow. I promise."

Kathy gave Deena a skeptical look. She had mixed feelings now about agreeing to this project, but she didn't want to get into a big fight with her cousin. Running a play group was harder than either of them had suspected, and they were both exhausted. Kathy decided to keep her misgivings to herself for now and see how it went tomorrow.

"I'm starving," she said. "Chasing those kids around really works up an appetite. Let's go have lunch."

*   *   *

The next day Deena and Kathy were more organized. The night before they had planned out several activities and games to keep the kids occupied. At first things went smoothly. Using the instruments Kathy and Deena had collected, the kids had a rhythm parade and danced to music on Kathy's boom box. After a game of Freeze Tag, Deena read them a story. Even Charlie sat still and listened until the end. However, shortly after Deena took out the finger paints, the orderly play group went wild. It all started when Brian and Todd decided to decorate each other like Indians on the warpath. Charlie soon joined in, and the three boys chased one another around the room.

"Look at them!" Deena screamed at Kathy. "How are we ever going to get them cleaned up before their parents come? Why did you let them do that?"

"I didn't *let* them do anything!" Kathy shouted back. "You were standing right here, too, you know. Why didn't you do something?"

Deena was about to reply when an unholy wailing sounded nearby. Dara and Kelly were having a hair-pulling fight. Deena left the boys to Kathy and ran across the room to break up the fight.

"O.K., you guys, calm down. Enough is enough," Kathy reprimanded the wild Indians. The boys ignored her and continued chasing one another around, over and under the furniture. Charlie had gotten hold of the big bag of cookies that were supposed to be served at snacktime. He opened it, stuffed two in his mouth at once, and then threw a fistful at Todd.

"Stop that! Give me back those cookies!" Kathy demanded, wrestling the bag away from him. Charlie stomped on her foot. "These kids are monsters!" Kathy shrieked, clutching the broken bag of cookies to her chest. "I don't want to do this anymore..."

"Don't you *dare* walk out of here, Kathy Ma-nelli!" Deena said, grabbing her cousin by the hem of her Springsteen T-shirt. "You're not leaving me alone in here all morning," she whispered through gritted teeth.

41

Even though Deena was trying her best not to make a scene, the children were instantly aware of the tension between the girls. They stopped chasing one another to watch Deena and Kathy fight.

"Deena—let go of me!" Kathy yelled, not caring whether or not the children heard her. "This whole stupid thing was your idea."

"And you *promised* you would be a partner!" Deena reminded her, refusing to let go of the T-shirt. "You can't just leave me here alone!"

"That's what you think." Kathy thrust the bag of cookies at Deena, who caught them in her free hand. "Just watch me."

She stubbornly turned and headed toward the door. Deena dug in her heels and tightened her grip on Kathy's shirt.

Kathy didn't get too far before a loud tearing sound stopped her in her tracks. She turned to see Deena with a huge piece of her T-shirt hanging from her hand.

"Bruce! You ripped Bruce!" Kathy wailed, twisting around to see the damage done to the back of her shirt. "Look at him! How could you?"

"Oh, stop. You sound like I murdered the guy or something," Deena said, beginning to see the humor in the situation.

The children laughed hysterically. It occurred to Deena that she and Kathy had finally succeeded in getting their full attention!

"It looks cool ripped," said Brian.

"This was my best T-shirt," Kathy went on furiously. "I got it at the greatest concert of my entire life. Do you know how hard it is just to get *into* a Springsteen concert? I'll never get another T-shirt like this one!"

"You have about a hundred of them, and they all look the same, if you ask me," Deena said airily. "Why don't you go inside and change. Then come back out, and we'll play another game. What do you want to play?" she asked the children.

"Freeze Tag—that was good!" Kelly shouted.

"Who wants Kathy to come back and play with us?" Deena asked.

"Come back and play, Kathy," Dara said sweetly.

They all wanted Kathy to come back—even Charlie. Kathy stood by the open door, her T-shirt flapping open in the back. She still looked angry, but finally she gave Deena a reluctant grin. "O.K., I'll be right back," she promised.

Deena was immensely relieved. She had a feeling she hadn't heard the last of her heartless treatment of Bruce Springsteen. But she knew Kathy wouldn't stay angry for long.

The rest of the session was uneventful. At noon, the parents came and collected their children. When the last one was gone, Deena lay down in the warm grass outside the playhouse and groaned aloud.

"I'd be making the same sound, only louder," Kathy said, flopping down next to her, "except I'm too tired."

"At least we made another twenty-five dollars to-day. Not bad for a morning's work."

"Sure—there are harder ways of making twenty-five bucks. Moving pianos, for instance. Taming wild animals . . ."

"Come on, Kathy. It wasn't as bad as yesterday . . . after we got the kids under control."

"After I tried to escape, you mean?"

"Well . . ." Deena looked up at her, shading her eyes from the sun with her hand. "At least you came back. I was afraid you wouldn't."

"I can't say the thought didn't occur to me," Kathy admitted with a grin. "But I knew it wasn't fair. Guess I just panicked. You know that Charlie stomped on my foot and nearly bit me when I finally got the cookies away from him? Besides—you owe me an apology for destroying my Springsteen shirt."

"I'm sorry. I didn't mean to rip it. But I was in a panic, too, when it looked like you were walking out on me," Deena explained, sitting up.

Kathy lifted her brown hair off her neck. "This play group business isn't going to be such a snap, Deena. I think my mom was right. This kid-watching stuff is harder than it looks."

"I know," Deena said quietly. "Does that mean you want to quit?"

"Well . . ." Kathy paused. "Do you?"

"I don't know. I'm exhausted and I have a splitting headache," Deena admitted, rubbing her forehead.

"I'm tired, too. . . . It got pretty wild there when

44

you yanked my shirt in half." Kathy laughed, recalling the expression on Deena's face.

"You should have seen the look on *your* face," Deena said, laughing now, too. "I would have done anything for a camera."

The girls sat back in the sunshine, laughing at each other.

"I owe you a T-shirt, O.K.?" Deena said finally.

"Oh—forget it. I guess I deserved it for trying to duck out like that." Kathy pulled up a dandelion and stuck it in the buttonhole of her blouse. "The thing is, Deena . . . I'm not sure I want to do this all summer. Even though we're making money, I don't know if it's worth it."

Deena felt her stomach scrunch in knots. She didn't want to start a big fight with Kathy, but she couldn't stand the idea of them giving up so quickly. "Look," she said. "I know it's going to be a lot harder than we thought, but you can't run out after only two days!"

Kathy slid her shades on. "I'm sorry, but I don't even remember why I agreed to do this in the first place."

"Something about being a role model for little kids?" Deena reminded her.

Kathy cringed inside, remembering the conversation at the dinner table a few nights ago. It had seemed like a challenge then to show how grown-up she was. Now it seemed like a total drag. Besides, the day before, someone at the beach had told her about the greatest

45

part-time job in the world at Slipped Disc, the record store in town. She hadn't planned to tell Deena anything unless she was hired, but Kathy decided that right now was as good a time as any to spring the bad news.

"Well . . . the thing is, I heard about this great job at Slipped Disc. The hours are eleven to two, so I can still help out at the inn before work and then hit the beach in the afternoon. And I'll get a great discount on records and tapes," Kathy rattled on excitedly. "I'm going over there today for an interview. If the manager hires me, I'm going to take it."

"Kathy—you can't just quit like this! It'll be easier tomorrow," Deena promised.

"You said that *yesterday*, remember? And why should it be any easier? We're getting two more kids to watch."

"It was much easier today than yesterday," Deena insisted, " . . . until the finger-painting incident," she added. "And besides, you're not supposed to leave a job without giving two weeks' notice."

"*Two* weeks? Who says?" Kathy thought she might offer to help out her cousin another day or two, until she could find somebody else. But two whole weeks? It sounded like an eternity.

"I read it in a magazine for working women," Deena said crisply. "Besides . . . I think your mother will be upset with you when she finds out you're quitting after two days."

Kathy knew what Deena said was true. She knew her mother still worried about the transition Kathy had

46

made after they had moved from California. She hadn't gotten the best grades in the world this year at her new school, and even though her mother now liked her boyfriend, Roy Harris, it had been rough going there for a while, too. She really didn't want to give her mother a reason for another major argument. She knew that if she stranded Deena now with the play group, her name would be *mud* at the Cranberry Inn. It looked as if she didn't have any choice but to stick it out for a while.

"All right, a deal is a deal. I guess I can stand it for two weeks," Kathy said finally. "I don't think the new job starts for a couple of weeks anyway, so I guess it will work out."

Deena sighed with relief. "Sure it will. It can't possibly be as awful as you imagine."

"*Nothing* could be," Kathy assured her. "But remember, whether or not I get that job, in two weeks I'm history. So you'd better start looking for somebody else to help."

"O.K., I promise," Deena reluctantly agreed. Secretly she thought there was a good chance that Kathy wouldn't get the job at the record store, and if Kathy didn't get the job she might have a change of heart and decide to stick it out for the whole summer after all. Besides, who could she get to replace her? If Kathy quit, that would probably be the end of the play group.

Chapter 4

As usual, Kathy went off to the beach for the afternoon. Deena, however, decided to hang around the inn. She was too tired to make the effort to go. Besides, she didn't want to risk running into that guy Davey again today. She was sure he was walking up and down the beach right now, looking for her with those hound-dog eyes. Well, he had a surprise coming. She would stay away from the beach for a week and maybe he'd find someone else to pester.

Deena got a glass of iced tea and settled herself in the swing on the front porch. For a while she just sat there, enjoying the shade and the lazy rhythm of the swing. Then, unable to be completely idle, she brought out a pen and some paper to write letters.

Deena decided to write her boyfriend, Ken, first. He was working as a counselor at a tennis camp, and even though he'd only been gone two weeks, she missed him.

She started the letter with some funny stories about the inn and the play group, and then some gossip about kids they knew at school—who was going out with whom this week. Then she asked him how camp was going and if he thought he might be coming home for a weekend sometime during the summer. She also told him that she was practicing her tennis, so he'd better be ready for some tough matches when he got home in August.

Deena finished her letter, giggling a little over the idea of giving Ken serious tennis competition. That meant she'd have to fit about ten years of practice into the next four weeks. Then again, she might just turn out to be a natural talent. She imagined playing a brilliant match and enjoying the look of surprise on Ken's face. Thinking about Ken, Deena realized with a pang just how much she missed him. She wished he hadn't gone away. They could have had so much fun together if he'd taken a summer job in town. It seemed so unfair that just when they had really begun to go steady, school had ended and Ken had left.

Deena still couldn't believe that Ken was actually her boyfriend. He was just so wonderful—smart, cute, incredibly athletic, and not the least bit stuck-up. How did she ever get so lucky?

Probably, she answered her own question, the way she'd just lucked into Dave Findlay. Some things were just meant to happen. But why Davey? He was the complete opposite of Ken. She genuinely felt sorry for him— but not sorry enough to hang out with him. Not for an afternoon. Not even for five minutes. What would her friends say if they saw them together?

"Deena, dear." Mrs. Culver, one of the guests at the inn, interrupted her thoughts. "Do you know what time the movie in town starts tonight?"

Generally, Deena liked the people who came to stay at the inn, but they all seemed to think that she and her family were walking encyclopedias when it came to movie and train schedules. Still, she always tried her best to be helpful, unlike Kathy, who usually gave one of her space-cadet grins and suggested the guests ask her mother.

Now Deena smiled at Mrs. Culver. "There's a movie schedule in today's paper. I'll get it for you." Deena went inside and brought Mrs. Culver the newspaper.

"Thank you, dear," said Mrs. Culver as Deena handed her the paper. "Why aren't you at the beach today?"

"Oh, I didn't feel like it, I guess," Deena said, not wanting to admit the real reason—that she was avoiding Dave Findlay.

"It *is* a bit hot," Mrs. Culver agreed, fanning herself with the newspaper. "Would you like to play some cards? Gin rummy?" she asked hopefully.

"Umm—I was just going to play tennis, practice my forehand a little," Deena excused herself. "Maybe another time."

"Of course. Young people like to keep moving.

Even in the heat," Mrs. Culver replied, opening the paper. "Have a nice tennis game, dear."

Deena went up to her room and got her racket and some tennis balls. Then she walked out to the old tennis court on the edge of the inn's property. The court was in pretty bad shape, since there wasn't enough extra money in the budget this summer to repair it. But the net was new, and there was a high wooden wall for handball, where Deena practiced her forehand when she didn't have a partner—which was just about all the time since Ken left for camp.

It was boring playing tennis against a wall all by herself. She had tried to get Kathy interested in the game, but had given up on that idea after one disastrous session. Still, she had promised herself that she would practice a few times a week, so that when Ken came back they could really have some good games.

Deena bounced the tennis ball, then whacked it into the wall. She was going to do fifty forehands, then fifty backhands.

"One," she counted out loud as the ball made a *thwack* sound against her racket. "Two..." *Thwack!* "Three..." *Thwack!* "Four..." She lunged for it, swung wildly, and missed.

Then, as she turned to retrieve it, the ball came flying through the air, returning magically under it's own power. Or so it seemed at first.

"Pull your racket all the way back, Deena," an all-too-familiar voice with a flat Iowa accent advised. "And don't take your eye off the ball right before you swing."

Deena caught the tennis ball as it bounced near her feet, then turned to face Davey with a hand on her hip. "Thank you, John McEnroe."

"Pretty hot out for tennis," he said, ignoring her wisecrack. "How come you're not at the beach?" Davey walked toward her with his hands in the pockets of his big baggy shorts. A green baseball cap was jammed on his head, and strands of his feathery blond hair stuck out from it in all directions.

"Why aren't *you* at the beach?" Deena countered. If it had been any other guy in town, she knew she would have hidden behind the nearest bush rather than let him see her looking so awful. She had on the same juice-splattered T-shirt and shorts she had worn for the play group, and her hair was pulled back in a messy ponytail. But with Davey, she considered her awful appearance an advantage. Maybe she'd scare him away, she thought hopefully.

Davey scratched at his neck. "I was just on my way. But I stopped by to see if you wanted to go. Some woman on the porch told me you were out here. She thinks it's pretty hot for tennis, too."

"So?" Deena shrugged. "I like to play tennis when it's real hot. My boyfriend, Ken, who's been teaching me how to play, says the heat loosens you up. He's a really good tennis player," Deena added.

There, she had said it. Now he knew for sure she had a boyfriend and wasn't interested in hanging out with him.

"Oh, yeah?" Davey didn't seem too impressed.

"You guys play together a lot?" he asked, his arms crossed over his chest.

"Well—not so much lately..." Deena debated whether to tell Dave the truth—that Ken was away. Then she chided herself for even thinking of lying to him. What difference did it make? Whether or not Ken was around, she still wasn't going out with Davey. "He's away for the summer working as a counselor at a tennis camp."

"Oh...too bad," Davey said with a big toothy grin. "Maybe you and I can play together sometime."

"You play tennis?" Deena asked, not really believing him.

"Sure—a little," he said with a shrug. He tugged nervously on the peak of his cap. "Think of it this way...no matter how bad I play, it has to be more fun than playing with the wall."

Deena couldn't help laughing. He did have a point, though. It was awfully boring volleying against the wall. Could she actually consider playing tennis with him? What if he thought it was a real date? But now he knew she had a boyfriend, she reminded herself. Well, maybe one of these days they could play together. It wouldn't be so terrible. If they were playing tennis, she didn't have to actually talk to him. Besides, she didn't want to be mean and give him a flat-out rejection.

"Sure, I guess we could play sometime," she replied vaguely, swinging her racket from side to side.

"We could?" Dave's face lit up. "How about right now?"

"Uh—right now?" Deena stopped swinging her racket and racked her brain for some semi-believable excuse that would get her out of this situation fast.

"Yeah—why not? Do you have an extra racket around I could use?"

"Umm—no," she said abruptly. "I'm the only one who plays tennis around here." There was Kathy's racket, and a few other old usable specimens in the garage that the inn kept on hand for guests. But Davey didn't have to know that.

"Really?" He looked surprised, but undaunted. "I'll go home and get my own. I'll probably play better with it anyway. Then maybe we could go for a swim. I'll grab a change of clothes. I'll just be a few minutes," he promised.

He was going all the way home, and then coming back again! And bringing some clothes! Deena couldn't figure out how she had gotten herself into this mess. All she'd said was that they could play *sometime*. She'd never invited him to check-in at the front desk.

"Hey—I think there are some old rackets in the garage," Deena said suddenly. "Maybe you can find one that's usable." She decided it would be easier to hit the ball around with him for a few minutes and then beg off because of the heat than to let him go home and come back again with a load of long-term sports supplies.

In the garage Davey picked out a racket. It was an easy choice since it was the only racket in the pile without any broken strings. The frame was hopelessly warped though, Deena noticed. She didn't think any player could tolerate using it for very long.

"Want to volley a little to warm up?" Dave asked as they walked back out onto the court.

"I'm pretty warm already, aren't you?" Deena said. She didn't want to prolong this match one minute longer than was absolutely necessary. "Let's just play."

"O.K. You can serve first," Dave said graciously.

"No—let's toss for it," Deena insisted. "That's the way it's done, you know."

"Yeah—I know," Dave said, with one of his goofy but admiring grins.

They spun Deena's racket, and it landed label up. Dave got to serve first.

"Mind if I take a few?" he called from the other side of the court as he adjusted his baseball cap. "I'm a little rusty."

Deena sighed with impatience, glad that he was so far away she could even complain about him out loud and he wouldn't hear.

"Go ahead!" she yelled across the court. "What a nerd!" she muttered aloud as she watched him get into position to serve. "He's probably the worst player on the eastern seaboard. Five minutes, and then I'm going to get a sudden case of heat—"

Dave's serve shot past Deena like a smoking bullet. Deena stared open-mouthed at the ball as it rolled behind her.

"Lucky sho—" she started to whisper to herself, just as his second serve, as wicked as the first, zipped by.

56

As Dave took two more serves on the other side of the court, Deena tried to appear unimpressed. Secretly she was feeling more than a bit confused. Could this guy actually be a passable tennis player?

A few minutes into the game, it was apparent that despite the handicap of a warped racket, Dave was the superior player. As Deena dashed frantically from one side of the court to the other to return his shots, she wondered what he played like with decent equipment.

He even looked different when he was playing, she noticed. His gawky, angular body, which normally seemed so clumsy and unsynchronized, moved with a fluid grace on the tennis court. As he rushed up to the net for a shot, Deena thought that for an instant he seemed *almost* passably cute . . . in a goofy sort of way.

After getting over her initial shock, Deena managed to hold her own on the court against him. They had each won a set, and Deena was content to quit with the tie score.

"I thought you said you could play 'a little'?" Deena said to him as they sat down on the grass in the shade of a big tree.

"I'm all right," Dave said with a modest shrug. "My mom is really a super player. She taught me how to play. You ought to see her on the court sometime. She could have been another Chris Evert Lloyd, I bet."

Deena thought it was nice the way Dave bragged about his mother being good at sports the way most guys bragged about their father or older brother. She thought he was unbelievably modest considering how well he played. And she could tell that it wasn't an act.

"I'd like to improve my serve," Deena confessed. "And my backhand isn't that great, either."

"You're not so bad," Davey replied, seeming surprised that she had put herself down. "You really had me on the run in that last game."

"Yeah—that was fun, wasn't it?" Deena said, recalling a particularly long rally which Davey had won with an impossible-to-return smash to center court. "That smash was a really cheap shot, though," she added.

"Sure was," he agreed, pulling his baseball cap back on. "But it worked," he added, making Deena laugh. "I can show you how to do that."

"Really? You could teach me that?" Deena would give anything to be able to make a shot like that the next time she played with Ken. She could already see the shocked look on his face.

"It's not so hard. The trick is to get the right timing. Want me to show you now?"

"Maybe another time," Deena said. She wanted to learn it, but right now she was really wiped out. "Let's go up to the inn and get something to drink."

"That sounds great." Dave looked ridiculously pleased by that idea. "Lead the way," he said, with a gallant flourish of his tennis racket.

Deena found a pitcher of iced tea in the fridge, and they sat out on the front porch while they drank it. Davey kept staring at her in his hound-dog fashion, and

Deena began to feel irritated by him again. They'd had an unexpectedly good time playing tennis, but now she wished he would drink his tea and go.

"There's a really good movie playing in town," Dave said suddenly, his voice cracking a bit as he spoke. "A murder mystery. I—uh—was going to see it tonight and was thinking that . . . that is, if you weren't doing anything, that maybe you would want to see it?"

"Sorry," Deena said, cutting in before he could manage to drag out the agony another moment longer. "I have to stay in tonight and wash my hair . . . and write a letter to my boyfriend," she added, hoping to remind him that just because they played tennis together, it didn't mark the start of any big summer romance.

"Oh—sure." Dave coughed and shrugged. He pulled his baseball cap off and bounced it on his knee. She could tell she had hurt his feelings, and she felt bad. But she didn't really know what to do about it. "I'm going for a swim, I guess," he said, finishing up his tea.

Deena held her breath, expecting him to ask her to come along to the beach. She was surprised and relieved when he didn't.

"It was fun playing tennis, Deena," Dave said as he stood up.

"Yeah, it was," she agreed, partly to be nice to him, and partly because it was true.

"Want to play again tomorrow?" he asked hopefully. "I could show you how to do that smash shot."

"Tomorrow? Gee—I'm not sure if I can play to-

59

morrow. . . . " she replied, not knowing what to say. She liked playing tennis with Dave, but she sure didn't want him to get the wrong idea.

"Well, I'll ride by and see if you're around," he said, pulling his baseball cap on again. The same tufts of blond hair stuck out over his ears. Deena restrained an urge to tell him pointblank how dumb it looked.

He hopped on his bike, gave her a brief wave, and was gone, leaving Deena feeling very confused. She had certainly had more fun with Davey this afternoon than she would have had by herself. Or even if she had gone to the beach with Kathy. He really wasn't so awful to be around when they were actually doing something, and he wasn't staring at her as if she'd dropped out of the sky.

And he sure could play tennis. She never in a million years would have admitted it out loud, but goofy Davey Findlay was almost as good a tennis player as Ken! If they played together for a few weeks, Deena knew her game would really improve. Wouldn't Ken be surprised when he got home and saw what a good player she had become?

Deena realized it was kind of shallow to want to spend time with Dave just so her tennis game would improve, but the truth was, she really didn't think he was so bad anymore.

Maybe they could be friends—if he could get it clear that she didn't want to date him. She just hoped she wouldn't have to hit him over the head with a tennis racket to get the point across. She had really been quite blunt about it today and had even turned down a date by saying she had to write a letter to her boyfriend. What more could a girl do?

Chapter 5

"So, did you find anybody to replace me yet?" Kathy asked Deena one night as she was getting dressed to go out. Over a week had passed since Kathy had given her "notice." She'd gotten the job at Slipped Disc and was planning to start working there next week. But Deena still hadn't done a thing about finding a new partner for the play group. Kathy didn't get it. "I don't know what you're waiting for."

"I'll find somebody," Deena said vaguely, glancing up from the book on tennis that she was reading. She was almost sure that at the last minute Kathy would change her mind. That's the way Kathy was: She said one thing and did another. "Maybe I should put a sign up on the bulletin board at the beach."

"That's a good idea," Kathy said, frantically brushing her spiky haircut. "Look at my hair! It's so horrible," she moaned, totally forgetting about Deena's hiring problem. "I can't go out like this!"

"What's wrong with it?" Deena asked, looking up from her book.

"What's wrong with it? It's a complete disaster! It's all over the place! It's horrendous!"

Which was exactly the way Kathy's hair always looked to Deena. However, seeing how upset Kathy looked, Deena was considerate enough not to say what she really thought.

"Why don't you try a clip?" she suggested. "Those strange ones you had on yesterday, you know, the ones that looked like they came from jumper cables?"

"They *are* from jumper cables," Kathy said as she rummaged around on top of her messy dresser looking for the hair ornament in question.

"Really?" Deena stretched and yawned. "Well, be careful you don't short-circuit your brain, Kath. We wouldn't want a total black-out up there."

Kathy glared at her cousin. "I'm having a fashion emergency, and all you can do is make fun of me. Thanks loads."

"Sorry," Deena said sweetly, "just trying to be helpful."

As far as Deena could see, every time Kathy got dressed it looked like a fashion emergency. Some days she didn't know how her cousin had the nerve to leave the house, but then, their taste in clothes and style could not have been more different. Deena's glamour ideal was Princess Diana. She would have done anything to have a wardrobe with all those gorgeous gowns, perfect dresses, and wonderful hats. Months ago Deena had stopped trying to give Kathy helpful hints about the way she dressed. Of course, the most helpful tip would be "Toss out everything in your closet and get your hands on an L. L. Bean catalog, pronto!"

Tonight Kathy wore a purple, flared miniskirt, with a huge black Nuclear Waste T-shirt tied in a knot at her waist, and pink ballet slippers that tied around the ankle. Deena noticed something that looked suspiciously like a dog collar wrapped around her wrist as a bracelet. As Deena expected, her earrings—all three of them—didn't match. There was a big silver star hanging from one ear, and on the other a silver loop and a bunch of dangling feathers that looked like a fishing lure.

"The clips definitely help," Kathy decided, stepping back from the mirror to survey the effect. "But I don't know now about the earrings . . . "

"Yeah—they are a bit much," Deena said, thinking that the hair clips made Kathy look like the Bride of Frankenstein, right before she gets zapped with a few thousand volts of electricity.

"What do you mean?" Kathy said. "I think they look too blah. Wait—I've got one that's perfect!"

She sifted through some junk on her night table and found what she'd been looking for—a bright pink plastic dinosaur hanging from a green earring wire. She pulled off the star and put on the dinosaur.

"There—now that looks like something," she said, finally sounding pleased with her appearance.

"Right—when the lab report comes back, let me know," Deena murmured, unable to resist. "By the way, what's the occasion?" She knew that Kathy couldn't be going to all this trouble dressing for a movie date with Roy.

"Oh, no big deal," Kathy replied lightly as she tossed half of the junk on her dresser into her huge purse. "It's only possibly *the* most exciting night of my life . . . that's all."

"Don't tell me." Deena put her book down and sat up. "You've finally figured out what planet you *really* come from and they're zooming in to take you home!"

"Was that a joke? I mean, am I supposed to laugh now?" Kathy replied dryly, tugging her purse over her arm.

"O.K.—I give up. Why is this possibly the most exciting evening of your life?" Deena knew it had to be good because Kathy, who didn't really confide much in Deena, looked as if she was so excited she might burst with the news.

"Things are really happening for Dementia," Kathy announced, referring to the band she was in. "Some people are coming to hear our band practice tonight, and they might hire us for a real job! Isn't that the greatest?" Kathy was so excited, her dinosaur earring was bouncing up and down.

"Sure," Deena said, thinking it would be great to go see Kathy's band play somewhere. "What kind of job? A party?"

"That's the best part, " Kathy explained. "We'd be

playing in the town square for the Founder's Day celebration. The town council is hiring all kind of bands to play all day at the big picnic. Everybody will hear us. We'll probably get loads of jobs after that."

"Wow—that would be terrific," Deena agreed, wondering what the town council members were going to think of Kathy's outfit. "Well, good luck."

"Hey, if you're going to make it big on the rock scene, it takes more than luck," Kathy said, sounding too hip to be believed.

"Right—really weird earrings are essential," Deena replied blandly. "And we *know* you've got that base covered."

"Oh, Deena." Kathy sighed with a somewhat superior manner. "What a wit! Or do I mean . . . what a twit?" she asked herself.

As Kathy sailed out the door, Deena realized that they had never talked over the plans for tomorrow's play group. Two more children were joining the group, which would bring the total up to nine. It would be a lot to handle, but luckily, things had been going much more smoothly the past few days. She and Kathy had learned a lot very quickly about how to handle children. At times she could almost swear Kathy was having fun—though she was sure her cousin would never admit it. Maybe Kathy would even find a way to take the job at the record store *and* stay with the play group for the summer. Of course, she'd probably always find a way to wiggle out of planning the activities. Deena had to admit that wasn't so bad, actually, since Kathy's ideas for activities were usually totally ridiculous.

Deena wondered what she could try that would hold the kids' interest. That was the whole trick. If you didn't capture their attention, you were in trouble. They really went haywire on you and then there was no getting them under control. For tomorrow, she decided they could make hand puppets with paper bags and then put on a puppet show.

Deena was writing down a list of things she would need for the project when she heard her mother calling her from the stairway, "Deena—there's someone here to see you."

"Oh, no," Deena moaned. She had heard that special tone in her mother's voice and knew it meant one thing—a boy was here to see her. She gave herself one guess: Davey Findlay. Deena sighed. What was she going to do about this situation? It wasn't enough that she had played tennis with him almost every afternoon. Now he wanted to hang out with her every night, too. She continued to sidestep his hints about movies, or going out for ice cream or a pizza. And she had made it perfectly clear that she had a boyfriend whom she was crazy about. None of this discouraged Davey, however.

Deena checked herself out in the mirror, but didn't even bother to comb her hair. She certainly didn't care what Davey thought of her looks! She could have sprouted a wart on the end of her nose and he still would have gazed at her with that moonstruck look on his face. More than anything else about him, it was that look that drove her straight up the wall.

Reluctantly, Deena went outside to the front porch, where she knew Davey would be waiting for her. He was sitting on the steps, but jumped up when he heard the door slam.

"Oh—hi, Deena. How are you doing?" he asked, sounding nervous and shy.

"I'm fine." Deena leaned against the porch railing, but didn't sit down. She hoped that if they didn't sit down, he wouldn't stay long.

"I hope I'm not bothering you or anything."

"Uhmmm . . . well, I was just working on something for my play group for tomorrow's session. I thought we'd try a puppet show."

Davey grinned. "That sounds like fun. What are you going to use for a stage?"

"Gee—I don't know. I haven't figured that part out yet."

Davey had a good idea about how to set up a little stage with a cardboard carton and a table. He started asking her more questions, and Deena found herself working out exactly what she and Kathy would do the next day.

As they were talking Deena realized that, unlike most other guys her age, Davey never seemed bored when she talked about her play group. Actually, he always sounded interested and came up with good suggestions.

"How do you know so much about putting on puppet shows?" Deena asked him curiously.

"During the school year I do volunteer work with handicapped kids," he said. "We do all kinds of things with them."

"Oh, that's really nice," she said, feeling suddenly ashamed of how much she complained to him about the kids in the play group. Dave must have real patience with kids if he could do that kind of volunteer work, she realized.

"It's O.K.," he said with a careless shrug. "Hey—I got another joke for you," he announced with a grin. "This one is really funny."

Deena sighed. "Go ahead."

"What do you call a haunted wigwam?" He waited a second, and grinned. "A creepy tepee." He laughed. "Funny, huh?"

"Yeah—that was O.K," Deena said, forcing a smile. She thought it was definitely time to go back inside and was about to say good night, but Davey spoke first.

"Hey—now that you've got your puppet show figured out, want to walk into town for some ice cream?"

So, tonight it was ice cream. She had to give him an "A" for effort, that was for sure. How many times did she have to say no before he'd give up? That was the question.

"Gee—I really don't feel like any ice cream, Davey," Deena said. "Besides, I have to wash my hair tonight."

"Oh. O.K." He was quiet for a second, and she thought he was about to say good night when he asked, "How come?"

"What do you mean?" she asked.

"Don't you like ice cream?"

"Well, sure I like ice cream. I like it a lot," Deena replied. "I'm just not in the mood for it."

"For someone who likes it a lot, you're never in the mood for it," Dave observed. "And the weird thing I noticed is that you have this strange reaction whenever I mention it."

"Strange reaction?" Deena asked, feeling flustered. "What do you mean?"

"Whenever I mention eating ice cream, it makes you want to wash your hair," Dave said innocently. "Really strange."

"That's not true," Deena said huffily.

"Oh, yes, it is," Davey said, nodding his head. "I've asked you every afternoon after tennis and almost every night for the past week. And you say, 'Sorry, Davey. I don't feel like ice cream. I have to wash my hair.' If you don't *like* ice cream, why don't you just say, 'Sorry, Davey. I really don't like ice cream'?"

The real reason Deena didn't want to go have ice cream with him was that she was afraid he would consider it a date. And to be perfectly honest, she was also afraid that anyone else who saw them would think the same.

Why did he have to be such a pest about it? Deena

71

thought angrily. She really tried to be nice to him, but this time he was pushing her too far. "I like ice cream fine," she insisted, crossing her arms over her chest. "The truth is . . . playing tennis once in a while is fun, Davey. I mean, I think you're a really nice guy and all. And I don't want to hurt your feelings, but"—Deena took a deep breath—"I don't want to go out on any dates with you."

There, she'd said it. She was sorry to have to be so blunt about it, but she sure felt relieved.

Dave just rolled his eyes. "Come on, Deena! I only asked you to go have ice cream. It wasn't exactly a marriage proposal, you know. Girls are so weird!"

"*Girls* are weird! You've asked me to have ice cream about ten thousand times. You'd think a person would get the hint. I already have a boyfriend, you know."

"I know! I know!" Dave tossed his baseball cap in the air and caught it. "Boy—do I *ever* know that you have a boyfriend. I think the whole world must know *that.*"

"Very funny," Deena said. She felt herself blushing and couldn't believe that this nerdy guy made her lose her cool. He really was such a stupid baby! "You really are a pest, you know that?" she said, feeling angry and embarrassed. "I wish you'd just leave me alone, O.K.?"

"Fine." Davey's voice was tight with anger. "I'm going. Don't worry, I won't take up any more of your *valuable* time. Girls like you always have a lot to do. Maybe after you wash your hair, you have to write your boyfriend the tennis champ another love letter . . . ."

"Maybe I do!" Deena said through clenched teeth. She whirled and ran into the house, slamming the screen door in Davey's face.

Chapter 6

Deena couldn't understand why she felt so bad after having her stupid little argument with Davey. But she did. She tried to just forget about it—and him. He was a jerk. A pest. A total nerd from Nerdsville. She really hadn't meant to be mean to him, but he'd pushed her into saying things that had hurt his feelings. Was that her fault?

A guilty thought wriggled around the back of her mind, telling her that perhaps she'd been taking advantage of his good nature. After all, she didn't mind playing tennis with him every afternoon. He really was a great tennis player and had already taught her a lot. They had fun together, too. But the idea of anyone finding out just how much she saw him made her hair stand on end. Wasn't that being rotten to a friend?

Deena tried to forget about the whole mess, but it kept nagging at her all the next morning, even during the play group. Although she and Kathy were busy every minute, helping the children put on the puppet show and handling two new additions to their group, Nancy and Mike, she couldn't get the fight with Dave out of her mind.

Kathy, however, was in a great mood. Her band audition had been a big success and she was floating on a cloud. Not even a roomful of noisy kids throwing puppets around could bring her down.

"O.K., I know you're all having fun. But it's time to go," Kathy announced to the children at a few minutes before twelve. "Let's put the puppets back in this box, and we can play with them again tomorrow."

Most of the kids did as they were asked, and a few minutes later their parents arrived to pick them up. Alone again, the girls began to clean up.

"Gee, this puppet show was a great idea, Deena. How did you figure out how to make this stage?" Kathy asked, looking over the converted cardboard carton.

"Uhmm—I don't know," Deena shrugged. "Davey told me how, I think." She gathered up a bunch of dirty paper cups and tossed them in the wastepaper basket.

"He did?" Kathy laughed. "You know, that guy seems like a real dope when you meet him, but under that nerdy outside . . . "

"There's an even nerdier inside," Deena finished for her. Today of all days she certainly didn't need to hear Kathy going on about how Dave was possibly a great guy in disguise. Like Clark Kent and Superman or something.

"If you say so." Kathy stared at her. "He's your friend."

"He is *not* my friend," Deena snapped. "He's a big pest, that's all."

"A big pest that you play tennis with every afternoon," Kathy reminded her.

"Not anymore. I told you, I don't like him, I don't want to look at his stupid face, or hear another one of his corny jokes ever again. If he calls, or comes here to see me, I'm not home."

"All right! All right!" Kathy said. "Gosh—you don't have to bite my head off."

"Sorry." Deena took a deep breath. Kathy, of course, had no idea that she'd had a fight with Davey the night before. "It's just that he was getting to be a real pain, and I told him to leave me alone," she added quietly.

"Oh, I get it." Kathy didn't know what to say. Deena claimed she despised the guy. Then why did she seem so upset? It was hard to tell someone to disappear, even if you didn't like them, Kathy thought. She'd been in that situation herself a few times.

"Well, if you think he's such a royal toad, you did the right thing, Deena. You can't hang out with a person just because you feel sorry for him."

"I guess so," Deena said. It was nice of Kathy to try and make her feel better, Deena thought, but somehow,

77

even though what Kathy said made sense, it wasn't any comfort.

"So since you're not playing tennis, want to go to the beach with me today and eat junk food and get mindless?"

"Sure." Leave it to Kathy to come up with that prescription for a bad mood. Maybe it would even work. "You wouldn't mind if I brought a book to read, though, would you? I mean, I wouldn't be embarrassing you in front of your friends or anything?" Deena teased.

"No problem. My friends already know how weird you are," Kathy replied lightly. "People have been asking me if you dropped off the face of the earth or something."

"Oh, really?" Deena made her tone casual. "What did you tell them?"

"I told them you were practicing for Wimbledon." Kathy shot her a sly glance as she piled a handful of crayons into a coffee can. "Don't worry, Deena. I didn't tell anyone *who* you were practicing with."

"I wasn't worried," Deena said with a shrug. She was relieved to know that Kathy had been surprisingly discreet.

But as Deena changed into her swimsuit she began to wonder what would happen if she ran into Davey at the beach today. Would he still be angry with her? Should she apologize to him for being so mean last night? Would he start pestering her again if she did?

For a moment she thought about staying home just to avoid seeing him. Then she got mad at herself. If she started thinking like that, pretty soon the whole town would be off limits. She wasn't going to let a silly misunderstanding with that creepy guy ruin her whole summer.

Kathy and Deena rode their bikes up the beach and found a spot for their towels near the water. For once, Kathy didn't immediately plug herself into her cassette player and start sunning herself like a human French fry. She was too busy spreading the big news about her band to all her friends on the beach.

"It's so exciting having a cousin who's *hallucinating* that she's a rock star," Deena murmured to herself as she pulled out a book from her tote bag.

Deena had decided to read only Hemingway novels this summer. She thought she might want to be a writer herself someday and knew she had to start preparing herself by reading all the classics. She had taken *A Farewell to Arms* out of the library. Kathy, of course, had wasted no time making fun of the title, facetiously asking what Hemingway had titled his other books—*A Good-by to Legs? An Aloha to Noses?*

Davey had said he'd read most of Hemingway's books, but he really liked Jack London better. They'd had a pretty lively argument about who was the better writer, she recalled. Deena turned the page, getting annoyed with herself for even thinking about him.

The afternoon passed quickly, and Deena became so engrossed in her book she forgot all about Davey. It was late afternoon when a girl from school, Cara Bates, walked up to her blanket and said hello. "Hi, Deena.

How's your vacation going? I haven't seen you around much."

"Oh, hi, Cara." Deena sat up and put her book aside. Cara was a year older, a cheerleader, and really popular at school. Deena knew her from the ski club, and also because she dated a boy named Mark Cutler, who was good friends with Ken. "I haven't been coming to the beach too much, I guess. I've been kind of busy. Kathy and I run a play group for kids at the inn."

"Really? All by yourself?" Cara seemed impressed. "I wish I'd found a job . . . but I guess I didn't look that hard," Cara admitted. "The summer is going kind of slow, just hanging out at the beach every day. I was thinking I might have a party soon. Just to liven things up. *If* my parents let me. They've really been on my case for coming in late at night, but that's the only time I get to see Mark." She smiled at the mention of her boyfriend. "Do you hear from Ken a lot?"

"We write each other almost every day," Deena said.

"Gee—that's really sweet. I wish a really cute guy like Ken were writing me letters almost every day," Cara said, sounding as if she thought that was the most romantic thing she'd ever heard. "I bet you really miss him."

"Yeah—I do," Deena admitted. "But he said he might be home for a weekend at the end of July . . . "

Just then Deena caught sight of Davey, standing by the water not too far away. He was staring at her and looked as if he might start walking toward her blanket. Deena stared back, then glanced back up at Cara, pretending she hadn't seen him.

But Cara had. "Oh, yuck! Do know that guy?"

"What guy?" Deena replied.

"That blond guy by the water. What a jerk!" Cara said. "He came over and started talking to me and Monica the other day. But we wouldn't have anything to do with him. I mean, he's really gross. He's from Idaho or something."

Iowa, Deena nearly corrected Cara. But she caught herself in the nick of time.

"Oh, him . . . I think I know who you mean," Deena said, hoping she could change the subject as quickly as possible. "Uhmm—did you ever read this book? It's really good," Deena held up her Hemingway novel.

Cara frowned. "I think I read that for English last year. It was really boring. Did you ever read *Sweet Winds, Wild Nights* by Vanessa Summerfields?"

"Uh, no . . . is it good?" Deena had never heard of the book, but she guessed that it was one of those trashy romance novels that were sold in the supermarket. The kind that always had some woman on the cover who had a lot of swirling hair and was floating on a cloud of pink flowers. She thought those books were just so stupid. Of course, she couldn't tell Cara that.

"It's really fantastic," Cara said. "Even better than her last book, *Wicked Winds, Stormy Nights*. Want to borrow it sometime?"

"Uh—sure," Deena said, not wanting to insult Cara by refusing such a generous offer. After all, it was a major social breakthrough having Cara Bates actually stop to talk to her for so long. Maybe they would get to be better friends this summer, and she would be part of Cara's crowd next year at school.

"Well, I've got to get going. See you around, Deena. Tell Ken I said hello when you write to him next time."

"I will," Deena promised. "See you."

When Deena glanced back at the shoreline, Davey was gone. She felt partly relieved and partly awful. She was glad when Kathy showed up a few minutes later and they decided to go back to the inn.

* * *

Deena hardly thought of Davey at all over the next few days—except for the afternoons when she was back to practicing tennis by herself against the boring wall. He didn't come to the inn, and she hadn't seen him at the beach, either. She wondered if he'd gone back to Iowa.

It was hard to be friends with a boy, she decided. Especially when he liked you more than you liked him. It was too confusing. She knew she'd be a lot more careful the next time something like this happened.

In the meantime, though, there were other, more urgent problems on Deena's mind. For one thing, with more guests arriving at the inn every day, the play group had more than doubled in size. They now had eleven children to take care of, and Kathy seemed to be losing

82

interest. All she thought about lately was Dementia. All she wanted to do was practice her songs, or think of new ones the band could play. They rehearsed almost every night, and she was so tired in the morning she could hardly get up.

Kathy had always imagined herself a rock star, but now she was really getting into the role. Almost unbearably so, Deena thought. And, of course, it really wasn't part of the hard-rocking image to be playing around with little kids every morning. Their two-week agreement was almost up, and Deena had a feeling that Kathy was going to quit after all.

The day before the two weeks were up turned out to be one of the hottest, and most difficult mornings in the history of the Cranberry Inn play group. Deena was trying to organize a game of Blue Bird outside, but every time she got the kids in a circle, one of them would start a fight or ask to be taken to the bathroom.

"I want my mommy," Lisa, the newest addition to the group, told Deena as she tugged on her T-shirt. "I want to go home now."

It wasn't even half past ten. Lisa was going to have to wait a while to see her mother. "It's not time yet for your mother to come and pick you up, honey," Deena patiently explained. "We're going to have a lot more fun this morning. We're going to play Blue Bird and do finger painting. And have juice and cookies . . . "

"I don't want juice and cookies," Lisa wailed, her face getting redder by the minute. "I want my mommy . . . "

"There, there. Don't cry." Deena knelt and put her arm around the little girl's shoulder.

While Deena comforted Lisa the other kids forgot why they were holding hands in a circle. They started wandering off in different directions. A few of the rowdier boys—Charlie and Justin and Henry Joseph—began throwing balls of rolled-up construction paper at one another.

"I have to go to the bathroom, Deena," a little boy named Sam insisted, somehow managing to make his voice heard over Lisa's crying.

"O.K., Sam. Hold on just a minute now," Deena said as calmly as she could under the circumstances.

"Deena!" Kelly shrieked, pointing to a scraped knee. "I hurt myself!"

Deena closed her eyes briefly, took a deep breath, then yelled, "Kathy!" But her cousin was nowhere in sight. She had gone back to the inn for the juice and cookies, promising she'd be back in a flash. That had been about twenty minutes ago. Some flash!

"Hi, Deena. What's going on here? Is this a play group—or a combat zone!"

It was Davey, holding a can of tennis balls and sounding as if everything between them was just fine.

Chapter 7

Deena couldn't think of anything to say except, "Davey—what are you doing here?"

"I wanted to return these tennis balls," he said with a shy shrug. "And talk to you, I guess."

"Oh—I'm sorry, Davey, but I really can't talk right now. It's a little crazy here . . ."

"So I noticed. Where's Kathy?"

"I don't know. She seems to have disappeared . . ."

"Deena—it's an emergency . . ." Sam warned her.

"What kind of emergency?" Davey asked him.

"The bathroom kind," Sam replied.

Davey looked at Deena, who was busy again with Lisa. And also Charlie, who claimed that Justin had socked him in the eye, and Kelly, who was holding Deena's leg and sobbing. "Hey, Deena, want me to . . ."

"Would you?" Deena said gratefully before he could even finish the question. "That would be great."

"Sure. Be right back." Davey took Sam by the hand and led him to the inn.

A few moments later Kathy finally reappeared.

"Where have you been?" Deena demanded.

"The cook served our juice for breakfast, so I had to make some out of frozen. I wasn't gone that long."

"Long enough—the kids are out of control," Deena said in exasperation. "Help me round them up, O.K.?"

A few minutes later they had gotten the kids to sit on the grass in a circle, though they had no idea what they were going to do with them.

Davey and Sam reappeared while the girls were talking over what to do next.

"I think we should play Blue Bird," Deena suggested. "They love that."

"They *hate* Blue Bird," Kathy said. "You're the only one who likes that silly game. Let's have an egg-on-a-spoon relay race. The winning team will get prizes."

"We don't have any prizes. And we don't have any eggs. And even if we got some eggs, they'd be wearing them in no time."

"Uh—Deena?" Davey was standing quietly to one side, listening to the two girls bicker.

"I'm sorry, Davey. Thanks for taking care of Sam, but I can't talk now. I'll call you, okay?" Deena said, barely glancing over at him.

Kathy came up with another one of her classic ideas. "Let's get one of the Spanish stations on the radio and make a conga line. I saw it in an old movie last night. The kids will love it! One of us will have to wear some fruit on our head, though . . . "

"A conga line! Are you out of your mind?"

Suddenly both girls stopped talking, both sensing at once that the kids were strangely quiet. For a single, hysterical instant Deena thought all eleven of them had gotten up and run off into the woods.

But when she spun around she heard them laughing. They were still sitting on the grass and staring in wide-eyed wonder at Davey. He stood in the middle of their circle juggling tennis balls.

"O.K.—now watch this," Davey said as he added a special variation, bouncing one of the balls off the top of his head every time it circled around.

"He's not bad," Kathy whispered. "I wonder if he knows magic tricks."

"I wouldn't be surprised," Deena replied.

"Let's ask him if he can make Charlie disappear," Kathy suggested.

Davey didn't make any of the children vanish, but he did make a coin pop out of one kid's ear and did some other tricks with a deck of cards that the children really loved.

Kathy served the juice and cookies, and Deena let them vote on playing either kickball, Hide-and-Seek, or Blue Bird. Kickball won unanimously, and Deena was glad Davey hung around to help out until the session ended at noon. He offered to help the girls clean up, but Deena wouldn't hear of it. He'd already helped them enough, she thought. She told him how grateful she was for all he'd done that day and promised to call him later in the afternoon.

Later, after he'd left, the two girls sank down on the lawn, exhausted.

"Dave is really incredible with kids," Kathy said, tugging on a blade of grass.

"He once told me he does volunteer work with handicapped children," Deena said.

"The kids really loved him. He's like a teenage boy version of Big Bird, know what I mean?"

"Yeah, he does look a little like Big Bird," Deena agreed. She wasn't trying to make fun of him. It was true.

"He's got loads of patience. Much more than I do," Kathy admitted.

"Oh?" Deena felt her stomach bunching up in a knot. Was Kathy trying to hint at something? "I think you're really good with the kids, Kathy. A lot better than when we started."

"You mean I haven't tried to escape lately?"

"Not just that. The kids really like you." In her own weird way, Kathy had a good rapport with the children, even though some of her ideas about how to entertain them were a bit bizarre. Deena still couldn't believe that conga-line business.

"I like them, too. They're all pretty cute. Except for Charlie maybe," Kathy added.

"One out of eleven isn't so bad," Deena cut in, sensing that Kathy was trying to tell her something she didn't want to hear.

"Listen, the thing is, I made a deal to stick this out for two weeks, and I've really tried to get into it, honestly, Deena." Kathy shook her head, her long bangs flopping in her eyes. "But I'm starting at Slipped Disc tomorrow, and you haven't done a thing about finding a replacement."

"I guess not." Deena didn't know what to say. Kathy had given her fair warning. But she had been so sure Kathy was going to change her mind. Deena shrugged apologetically. "I guess I didn't think you would really go."

"Sorry, but you should have believed me." Kathy caught herself as she saw how downhearted Deena looked. "Hey," she said softly, "don't look so bummed out. I'm sure you can find someone else to help you run the play group. Somebody who would probably be a whole lot better at it than me."

"Like who? Who am I going to find now, in the middle of the summer?"

"Gee—I don't know . . . " Kathy stared into space for a long moment and Deena was sure she was going to suggest something like sending the kids off in groups of three to form their own rock bands. "I know!" Kathy said excitedly. "Davey can replace me!"

"Davey! Are you crazy? I can't ask Davey to do it with me!"

"Why not? He was great with the kids. And you know he'd do it if you asked him. Probably for free, too," Kathy added with a sly grin. "Just to be near your wonderfulness . . . "

"Don't be ridiculous," Deena snapped. "I'd never ask him to do it for free. We'd be partners, just like you and me. Not that I'd ever ask him in a million years to do it," she added quickly.

"But why not? I don't get it, Deena. I mean, I know he's a nerd and all . . . "

"It's not that. I mean, he's not really such a nerd. Well, he is, but not in a really awful way. I mean . . . I don't even know what I mean," Deena said, feeling confused.

Why did this have to happen just when they had gotten so many kids in the group and were really rolling along? Couldn't Kathy stick it out for a few more weeks? Deena asked herself. Why did she have to find a stupid job in a record store?

Kathy stood up and stretched, clearly having settled the matter in her own mind. "Well, sorry to say it, Deena, but I think Big Bird is your only choice. Even if he's been a pest about wanting to date you. But maybe you guys should just have a talk. I mean, I know you're irresistible and all," she added, "but maybe he doesn't even have as big a crush on you as you think."

Leave it to Kathy to do wonders for my ego, Deena thought. "Right—I guess boys do find me pretty forgettable," she said sarcastically.

"Hey—that's not what I meant at all," Kathy said. "Oh, you know what I mean. I think you should ask him to take my place. I think it would really work out fine."

"O.K., O.K. I'll think about it." Deena picked up

90

the tennis balls and tried to juggle them. They bounced off in all directions.

Life was sure strange. A week ago she never wanted to speak to Davey again. Now here she was, actually thinking of asking him to take Kathy's place in the play group. She knew he would probably agree to work with her.

But Deena wondered if she'd be taking advantage of him. She knew how much Davey liked her. Would it even be fair to ask him to help out? It was confusing.

He'd been so nice and helpful today; it had really been fun to have him around. Maybe Kathy was right, Deena thought as she gathered up the tennis balls. Maybe if she and Davey talked things over they could work together and just be friends.

Kathy left for her band practice right after lunch. It took Deena a while to psyche herself into calling Davey, but finally she dialed his number.

"Hi, Davey—it's me, Deena," she said when he answered.

"Oh—hi, Deena. Have you recovered from the kickball game yet?"

"The kids were pretty wild, weren't they? They're not like that usually."

"Oh, they weren't so bad," he said.

"Well, thanks again for helping us out. I bet you didn't expect to get stuck working this morning when you dropped by."

"Well—not exactly. I came by early because I knew you'd be there, though," he admitted. "And, like

I said, well . . . I did want to talk to you," he stammered, sounding nervous.

"I wanted to talk to you, too," Deena managed. She twisted the phone cord around her hand. "But you go first . . ."

"That's O.K. . . . you can go first. What did you want to talk to *me* about?"

"It's no big deal. Well, I wanted to ask you about something. But I'd rather you told me why you came over this morning," Deena said, suddenly thinking that maybe he didn't like her as much as she thought after all. Maybe he had come over to tell her she was pretty awful to chase him off her porch and then snub him at the beach.

"Well—" Deena heard him take a deep breath. His voice sounded suddenly croaky. "I was talking to my dad the other night, about what happened when I asked you to go for ice cream last week? Remember?"

"Sure—I remember," Deena said.

"And, well—I wanted to apologize. That's all."

"Apologize?" Deena was really surprised. "What are you apologizing for?"

"Because you were right. I was being kind of a pest," Davey said, suddenly laughing at himself. "I get like that sometimes," he admitted shyly. "I know I do."

"How could you apologize to me? I was really horrible," Deena said. "I mean, I didn't have to yell at you."

"Yeah—well, sometimes I don't hear very well," Davey joked. "Especially when it's something I don't want to hear. Like my dad telling me to clean up my room. Or, say, a friend doesn't want to do something I want to do ... know what I mean?"

"Yeah," Deena said, understanding that he was trying to tell her that he wasn't going to pressure her anymore. "Everybody does that once in a while."

"Well." He took another breath. "I really like being friends with you, Deena. But I think I kind of screwed it up. Couldn't we play tennis again sometime? You know, when you aren't busy?"

"I like being friends with you, too, Davey," Deena admitted. She meant it, too.

"You do?" he asked, sounding surprised and happy. "I mean, really?"

Boy, he was a goofball sometimes, Deena thought. But now his astounding modesty was beginning to seem like a very special quality.

"Listen, here's what I wanted to ask you ... " She quickly explained that Kathy was taking a job in a record store and that she really needed someone to take her place in the play group. "I don't want you to say you will if you really don't want to do it," she finished. "But do you think you would be interested in being my new partner?" Deena crossed her fingers, hoping he'd say yes.

"Wow! That would be great!" From the other side of the phone it sounded to Deena as if he'd jumped out of his chair and knocked it over. "When do I start? This is the greatest. Wait till I tell my dad ... "

"I guess you can start tomorrow if you want," Deena said, feeling relieved and happy herself. "Kathy will be thrilled to find out she can sleep late."

"Hey, maybe I'll bring my banjo tomorrow. Kids really like that."

"You play the banjo, too?" Deena asked.

"A little," he said, sounding suddenly self-conscious.

"Like you play 'a little' tennis?" she teased.

"Oh, I'm O.K. I can play a few songs. Nothing that great," he said in a rush.

"Want to come over? We can plan out some things to do with the kids this week," Deena suggested. Finally she had a partner who would have some practical ideas about how to keep the children occupied. No conga lines, either.

"Sure—I'll be over in a flash. I'll bring my tennis racket, too. O.K.?"

"Of course," Deena said lightly. "I have to warn you, though. My backhand is really a mess this week. I don't know what I'm doing wrong."

"I'll help you with it," Davey said. "I mean, what are friends for, right?"

"Right," Deena agreed, feeling that things might work out even better than she had planned.

Chapter 8

What had seemed for a moment like an absolute disaster had turned out to be best for everyone. Kathy adored her job at Slipped Disc, and as she had predicted, Davey was the perfect partner for running the play group. He took on the job with an energy and enthusiasm that Deena found quite contagious.

From the very first day, Deena could see that Davey was more comfortable with the children than her cousin had been. Now that she was partners with him, running the sessions seemed a lot less chaotic. The mornings went faster, and it *certainly* was more fun.

A few days after Davey started work, they took the kids on a nature walk in the woods. Deena led the way. "Walk *very* softly, now," she told them in a hushed voice as they began the trail. "Like Indians."

"We don't want to scare the wild animals," Davey added.

"Are there any ferocious bears in here?" Charlie, the monster, wanted to know.

"Could be," Davey replied in a very serious tone. For once the little guy looked as if he might behave himself, and Davey couldn't resist encouraging his fantasy. "I think you'd better hold on to your partner, Charlie, and be extra quiet so we don't wake any of them up."

Although they didn't see any animals quite as impressive as a bear, they did come across a doe and her fawn. The animals disappeared in the blink of an eye, but not before the children got a look at them. Davey and Deena pointed out other, less obvious sights: a chipmunk scampering into a hollowed-out tree, a salamander sleeping on a rock, a fallen tree trunk covered with wild mushrooms.

The kids returned to the playhouse with a varied collection of wild flowers, bird feathers, leaves, seeds, and stones. Deena asked them to leave everything on a table in the playhouse before they went home. She thought it would be fun to have a show-and-tell the next day and teach the kids a bit about what they had found.

"Hey, Deena. Did you see this cocoon?" Davey asked as he sorted through their treasures. He held up a long black twig with a puffy white wad stuck in the fork of two branches. "Charlie found it. I wonder what's inside."

"As long as it isn't ferocious bears, I don't think he'll be too concerned," Deena said with a laugh. "Maybe it will turn into a butterfly."

"Yeah—maybe. That would be really neat."

Davey gently turned the branch so that they could look at it. "It's really neat the way something strange and creepy, like a caterpillar, can sprout wings and turn into a butterfly."

"I know what you mean," Deena said, staring down at the cocoon. "Once you know where butterflies come from, you can never really look at a caterpillar the same way."

"I hope whatever is in there pops out," Davey said, carefully placing the cocoon in a jar and putting it on the window sill. "We'll have to wait and see."

The afternoon promised to be one of the hottest they'd had all summer, and Davey said he was going straight to the beach for a swim. "Want to come with me?" he asked Deena.

"O.K." It really was too hot for tennis. "I'll go put on my suit. I'll be right down," she told him.

Up in her room Deena had a sudden flash of apprehension. Was she actually going to hang out with Davey in public? What would people think of her? She'd gotten so used to his company these last few days, she'd stopped thinking of him in the old way. Somehow she didn't even see the geekiness anymore. Just a new friend.

It really was selfish and shallow, Deena knew, to be thinking mean thoughts of Davey now. And even worse, worrying what people would think when they saw her hanging out with him. She gave her hair an impatient stroke with the brush. She was going to the beach with a good friend—that's all there was to it.

As usual, Deena and Davey rode to the beach on their bikes. Even from the bike stands, Deena could see that the beach was crowded.

"Gosh," said Davey as they tramped along the sand, looking for a place to settle, "it looks like everyone in town is here today."

"Sure does," Deena agreed. Everyone I know from school anyway, she added silently with a twinge of dread.

Walking beside Davey, she'd already passed a few groups of kids she knew. They all looked dazed from the sun and so far nobody had waved hello. But she knew it was only a matter of time until somebody noticed her.

When they had spread out their towels on the sand, they decided to go swimming right away. Deena, as usual, went in as slowly as possible. She liked to take her time getting used to the chilly water. Davey surfaced beside her with a splash, and laughing, Deena gave up and dived in. The water felt great, and for a while she forgot all about her problems.

"I'm really hungry," Deena announced when they finally came out of the water. Davey had eaten at the inn before they'd left, but she hadn't been hungry then. "I'm going up to the snack bar. Want anything?"

"Hmmm—I don't know. I did have a sandwich before."

"Correction—you had your sandwich and mine," Deena teased. Davey had the most amazing appetite she'd ever seen. He could eat and eat, and never seemed to gain an ounce on his beanpole body. Boys were just luckier that way, it seemed. Sometimes she couldn't help bugging him about it. "How about a small snack— a pizza perhaps?" she suggested dryly.

"What are you getting?"

"A chili dog, I think. And French fries."

"I think I'll just have a soda," he said after thinking it over. "I'm really in a banana split mood today. But I'll wait till later."

"When you're feeling weak from hunger, you mean? Getting dizzy, feeling faint, seeing spots in front of your eyes..." Deena elaborated in a dramatic voice.

"Yeah—in about fifteen minutes or so," he replied, checking his watch. "Want me to walk up with you?"

"No, that's O.K. I'll be right back." Deena got some money out of her wallet and put on her sunglasses and a T-shirt.

The snack bar was packed, and Deena stood at the end of a long line, waiting to order.

"Hi, Deena. How's it going?" Cara Bates came into the snack bar and got in line right behind her.

"Oh, hi, Cara. How are you?" Deena said with a smile.

"You know." Cara shrugged. "Just hanging out. This summer is going really slow. Hey, I heard your cousin's band is going to play at the Founder's Day picnic. Pretty neat."

"Yeah, Kathy's really excited. Well, maybe excited

isn't quite the word. She's more like hysterical," Deena replied.

"I'd be, too—wouldn't you? Getting up in front of all those people. I guess it's almost like being a cheer-leader." Cara flipped her long hair back with her hand. "But when you cheer, you're just shouting stuff out in a group. It's not like really singing."

"Believe me, what Kathy does isn't really singing, either," Deena joked. Actually, Deena thought Kathy was really talented. But she couldn't understand her cousin's taste in musical styles. "It's more like just shouting stuff out in a group. With electric guitars," she explained.

"Oh—right," Cara replied. She snapped her chew-ing gum. "My parents finally said I could have a party. I think they decided it was better to give me permission than for me to have one anyway when they went away on vacation. But it's going to be a serious trash night anyway," she promised Deena. "Maybe I'll ask your cousin's band to play. Think they would charge a lot?"

"I could ask Kathy for you," Deena offered. Gosh, a party with a live band and everything. It did sound great. Deena had never been to any party that could even vaguely qualify as a trash night, much less a serious one.

Everybody knew that Cara and her friends gave the best parties of any group at school. It would be really fun to go, Deena thought. She wondered if Cara was going to actually invite her. But why else would she even talk to her about it, if she wasn't invited? Still, Cara hadn't actually asked her to come yet.

"Hey, I saw that creepy guy Davey sitting with you before." Cara snapped her gum again and made a face. "I hope he doesn't come over to my blanket and bother me. How did you get rid of him?"

Deena was tongue-tied for a moment. The line had moved up, and she busied herself taking a plastic tray off the pile and grabbing a handful of plastic knives and forks and some straws.

"I didn't get rid of him . . . We're kind of sitting together. I mean, we kind of came, you know at the same time," Deena admitted in a rush. "Can I have a chili dog, large fries, and two Cokes?" she shouted to the boy behind the counter without even glancing at Cara to check her reaction.

There, I've said it, Deena thought with relief. She isn't going to stop liking me just because I'm friends with Davey.

"What do you mean? Did he follow you in from the parking lot or something?" Cara asked quite seriously. "Why don't you get the lifeguard to tell him to go away?"

As Deena's food came sliding across the counter toward her, she realized that she'd completely lost her appetite.

"Ask the lifeguard? No, it wasn't like that," Deena said, feeling frazzled. "I mean, we came together. On purpose."

"Like on a date on purpose?" Cara looked like she was about to burst out laughing.

"It isn't a date," Deena said, beginning to get mad. What difference did it make to Cara if it was a date? "We're just friends."

"You're friends with him?" Cara looked almost as appalled at the notion of Deena being friends with Davey as she had at the idea that they were dating.

Deena felt as if she was being interviewed by Barbara Walters. She knew that whatever she told Cara would be broadcast all over the beach in a matter of minutes. And Cara was staring at her as if she'd caught some really gross disease.

"Well, not friends, exactly," Deena said nervously. "Davey and I are working together. My cousin got a job at Slipped Disc, and he took her place in the play group I told you about."

"Oh," Cara said. "I guess that makes sense. He's definitely the type of guy that's into babysitting." She looked suddenly apologetic. "I didn't really think you'd go out with some super nerd like that, Deena. Honest."

"That's O.K.," Deena said.

Cara started talking about her boyfriend's new car and how she couldn't wait to get her license next summer. Deena nodded, not really listening.

She felt creepy all of a sudden. She knew she should have spoken up for Davey, but she didn't have the nerve. Why couldn't she have admitted that they were friends? Because she was such a total coward, she told herself bitterly. She stepped away from Cara and made a silent vow. "I will never do that again," she promised herself. "Davey is my friend and I'm not going to deny it. No matter who asks me."

Deena had an impulse then to tell Cara what she really thought of Davey—that once you got to know him he was a really neat guy, and that they had become good friends over the past few weeks. But she didn't have the chance, because suddenly she saw Davey walking away from the cashier with a banana split. She smiled and tried to catch his eye, but he didn't look her way.

"Oh, there's Davey," Deena said to Cara. "I think I'll catch up with him. See you later."

"Sure. See you," Cara replied.

"Hey, Davey," she called out. "Wait up."

"Oh, hi," he stopped and turned. "I—uh, didn't even see you in there."

"I guess you were hungrier than you thought," Deena said, glancing down at his huge ice-cream sundae.

"Oh, yeah . . . I guess," Davey replied vaguely.

"Why don't we find a table and sit down?" Deena suggested, glancing around for an empty spot. What was wrong? Davey didn't sound like himself. Was he nervous with so many kids from Deena's school around, looking at them?

Or had he heard her talking to Cara, denying that

she was his friend, all but agreeing that no girl in her right mind would ever go out with him? Deena felt her stomach curl up in a knot.

They found a table and sat down. "Here's your soda," Deena said, handing Davey his soda and straw.

"Thanks."

She took a bite of her chili dog and glanced up at him. He was poking his banana split with a spoon, but so far he hadn't eaten any of it.

"You want some of these French fries?" Deena asked. "I'll never finish them all."

For the average person, the idea of eating French fries and a banana split would have been un-appetizing, to say the least. But Deena knew that Davey, whose stomach was a lot like a trash com-pactor, wouldn't have thought there was anything odd about the combination. That's why she was surprised when he refused.

"Uh—no thanks," he said. He began to take a big bite of his sundae, then put the spoon down. "I don't know . . . I don't think I'm so hungry after all . . . I don't feel well," he said suddenly.

Deena looked up at him. He did look pale—not quite himself.

"What's the matter? Do you feel really hot? Want me to get you some ice water?" She tried to remem-ber her first-aid course. Maybe he'd been out in the sun too long. "Maybe we should walk over to the life-guard office," she suggested, feeling concerned about him. If he was passing up a banana split, it had to be serious.

"Uh—no. I don't want to do that. I think I'll just go home."

"Do you feel well enough to ride your bike? We can call your dad. Or maybe my mother can come and get us."

"I can ride home. I'll be O.K.," Davey said. He stood up. "You want this?" he asked, glancing down at the banana split.

Deena shook her head. "No, thanks." She didn't feel like eating anything, either. What was wrong with Davey? Was he really sick, or did he just want to get away from her?

Davey tossed his sundae in a nearby trash can. "I'm going to get my stuff. See you tomorrow, Deena," he said, walking away.

"Wait—I'll ride back with you," Deena said. She tossed the food left on her tray in the trash, too, and ran to catch up with him.

"You don't have to. It's O.K.," he said.

Something in his tone told Deena he really didn't want her to ride back with him. They walked back toward their towels without talking. She felt worse than ever, but she didn't know what to do.

Davey quickly gathered up his things. "See you," he said, pulling his green baseball cap low over his eyes.

"I'll call you tonight to see how you are," she told him. "Hope you feel better."

"Thanks." Davey glanced at her over his shoulder, then looked straight ahead as he began to walk up to the parking lot.

Deena watched him walk away, weaving his way through the crowd until all she could see was his green baseball cap. Then she lost sight of him entirely.

She turned and stared out at the water. She didn't know why she should feel so rotten all of a sudden, but at that moment all she wanted to do was cry.

Chapter 9

D eena called Davey that night, but his father answered the phone and said he was sleeping. "It's probably too much sun, or a bug of some kind," Mr. Findlay explained. "But I don't think he'll be coming to work tomorrow, Deena."

"Oh—sure. That's O.K.," Deena said. "I'll call him tomorrow. I hope he feels better. Would you tell him that?" she asked Davey's father.

"Sure. I'll give him the message," he promised.

Deena said good night and hung up the phone. She sat in the dark at the top of stairs, feeling even worse than she had at the beach. For one thing, she didn't know if she could run the play group all by herself. The truth was, the very thought of it terrified her. But that didn't seem too important compared to Davey. Was he really sick? she wondered. Or were his feelings hurt? Maybe he just needed some time by himself.

Deena went into her bedroom and flopped down on the bed. Kathy was rehearsing with her band again tonight and wasn't home yet. Usually Deena loved to spend time alone in the room they shared. But tonight she felt lonely. Even Kathy's bizarre conversation would have been preferable to her own unhappy thoughts.

Davey couldn't keep saying he was sick indefinitely, she reasoned. He'd probably be back at the inn by the day after tomorrow, and when she saw him again, she would ask him if there was anything that he wanted to talk about. Deena would find out for sure if he had overheard her. Then they would clear the air. She would apologize for being so horrible, and everything would be smoothed over. A day wasn't so long to wait, she thought.

* * *

Deena had a rough time handling the children all by herself the next day. Luckily, there were all the natural treasures the kids had found in the woods to talk about. Deena did her best to make the show-and-tell time interesting, but she couldn't help thinking how much better it would have been with Davey there.

The children missed him, too, and asked Deena a few times where he was and when he was coming back.

"He stayed home today because he doesn't feel well," Deena explained to them. "But he'll be back tomorrow."

He will, too, Deena told herself. But that afternoon, when she called Davey's house, she began to doubt that he'd be back the next day. Or any day.

The phone rang about ten times before Davey picked it up. "Hello?" Deena heard him say in his croaky voice.

"Hi, Davey. It's me, Deena," she said. "I called you last night, but you were asleep. How do you feel today?"

"Ummm—well, not great," he said. "I still feel . . . kind of bad."

"Oh—I'm sorry." Deena wondered if there was anything she could do. Should she just ask him if he was really sick? But if he was sick, the question would sound as if she thought he was faking. She didn't know what to do. "The kids all asked about you," she said then. "They really missed you."

"Oh, really? They did?" he said, sounding a little more cheerful. "How did it go? Did they behave all right for you?"

"They were O.K., I guess," Deena answered slowly. "But I wouldn't want to be alone with them every day."

"I guess not," Davey said, sounding distracted. "Listen, I'd better get off the phone. I—uh—don't think I'll be coming tomorrow, Deena."

"Sure, that's O.K.," Deena said. "Just get better. I'm going to the library today. Do you want me to get any books out for you?"

"No, thanks. I've got plenty of stuff to read here. I don't feel much like reading anyway."

109

There was a long silence. Deena tried to summon up the courage to ask him if he was really sick or mad at her.

"Davey—" she began.

"Listen, Deena, I have to get off the phone now. I'll talk to you sometime. Over the weekend, I guess," Davey said abruptly. He hung up before she could even say good-by.

Deena sat staring at the phone, wondering if she should call him back. Then she thought maybe she should ride her bike over to his house. Would that be better? she wondered. Or should she call him back later tonight? As she debated how to handle the problem, the phone rang. She picked up immediately, expecting to hear Davey's voice on the other end of the line.

"Hello?" she said eagerly.

"Hi, Deena. It's Cara."

"Oh, hi, Cara." Deena felt flustered. Cara had never called her before. "What's doing?"

"I wanted to invite you to my party," Cara said. "It's kind of last minute. My parents said I had to have it this weekend or not at all. It's Saturday night. Think you can come?"

"Saturday? Sure, I'd love to come," Deena replied. She was surprised that Cara had decided to invite her after all.

After Deena took down Cara's address and phone number, the two girls said good-by. The idea of going to one of Cara's superior trash nights did lift her spirits.

The attention from someone who was so popular at school made Deena feel good. For a moment Deena thought that if Davey didn't come back to the play group, she might ask Cara if she wanted to work with her. Cara was always complaining about being bored and having nothing to do but hang out.

Deena immediately dismissed the idea. She didn't want Cara to take Davey's place. She wanted Davey to come back. Cara wasn't her friend. Not really. When Deena thought about Cara now, she realized that since she'd gotten to know her better, she really didn't admire the older girl as much as she had before.

Cara really was kind of . . . well, shallow, Deena thought. Even the books she read were really bubble gum for the brain. And Cara had been so mean about Davey, and she didn't even know him, Deena thought.

Oh, really? Look who's talking, a little voice chided her. You're the one who denied being friends with him, her conscience reminded her. Talk about shallow.

Deena went out and practiced tennis for the rest of the afternoon. To keep her mind off her worries, she forced herself to hit a hundred forehands, backhands, and serves. She had really improved the last few weeks, and she didn't have to remind herself why.

* * *

Handling the play group alone the next day was really difficult. Not just difficult, Deena thought, impossible. The kids wouldn't listen to anything she said. They ran around, shrieking and bouncing off the walls,

111

knowing she couldn't possibly control all of them. She was scurrying in all directions at once, sure that one of them would get hurt.

They only quieted down to ask about Davey. "You said Davey was coming back today," Charlie reminded her.

"Well—I thought he'd be better. But I guess he's still sick," she explained, not knowing what else to say. "Look, I have a good idea. Why don't we make Davey a get-well card? Maybe it will cheer him up."

The children thought that was great idea. For the first time all morning Deena was able to get them under control. Well, almost under control. At least they were all in the same place at the same time. They made Davey's card on a huge sheet of paper that Deena had bought at a crafts store, thinking the kids would make a mural. But using it for a card for Davey seemed an even better idea.

They all sat on the floor, each child staking out a section of the paper for their own message to Davey. They used paint, felt-tip markers, crayons, and cut-out pieces of construction paper. It was really quite beautiful when it was finished, Deena thought. A real work of art, created from the heart.

"But how will he get it?" Lisa asked Deena. "It's too big to fit in the mailbox."

"Don't worry," Deena said, laughing. "I'll take it over to him myself. Special delivery," she promised.

After the children left, Deena rolled up the card and tied it with a big ribbon. It was too large to fit on her bike, so she decided to walk over to Davey's house with it. She thought about calling first, but then she got a fluttery feeling in the pit of her stomach. Their phone conversations hadn't been the greatest lately. What if he told her not to come over? No, it was better to surprise him, she decided.

It was a sticky, overcast day, and the weather report had promised thundershowers in the afternoon. Deena hoped she wouldn't get caught in the rain. She wasn't worried about getting wet, but she didn't want the card to be ruined.

When she finally reached Davey's house, Deena was hot and sweaty and a little bit scared. What if he wouldn't see her? She walked up to the front door and rang the bell. She thought she saw the curtain move upstairs, but she wasn't sure.

She waited, but nobody answered. Putting the card aside, she knocked hard. "Davey?" she called out through an open window. "Anybody home?"

She waited again. She had the oddest feeling that Davey was in there, but he just didn't want to see her. Finally, Deena decided to leave the card and try to call him later. But she couldn't leave it out front, she realized. It was going to rain any minute, and the card would be ruined. She walked around to the back of the house, hoping to find a covered porch or awning.

At the back of the house there was a wooden deck and a table covered by an open sun umbrella. Deena propped the roll of paper up against the umbrella and tied it to the stand with the ribbon. She was just walking off the deck when she realized the back door of the house was open. She peered in through the screen.

"Davey? Are you home?" she called out once more. She waited, sensing that he was standing nearby in the shadows and had heard her.

"Yeah—I'm home," said a quiet voice. Davey came into the kitchen and opened the door.

"Hi," Deena said. "I knocked before . . . I guess you didn't hear me."

"I guess not," Davey said, averting his eyes. "What are you doing here?"

"I brought you something. The kids made you a big card. It's on the table outside," she explained. "It's really great."

"Oh—thanks. That was really nice of you to bring it over." He glanced outside and saw the card, but didn't make any move to go get it.

"How are you feeling?" Deena asked, trying to draw him out. "You look better."

"I'm O.K.," he said with a nod. "But I don't think I want to come back to the play group anymore, Deena. I'm sorry but . . . " He shrugged. "I just don't know."

"Oh." Deena didn't know what to say. She felt terrible. "You're mad at me, aren't you?"

Davey looked surprised. "Why do you say that? What do I have to be mad at you about? I—umm—just don't want to do the play group anymore, that's all."

"You heard me talking to Cara about you the other day at the beach, didn't you?" Deena finally managed to say. The look on his face told her that her worst fears were true.

"Yeah—I did." He nodded, looking down at the floor. "I know you didn't want to go out with me . . . I didn't care about that so much anymore, honest. But I thought you were my friend . . . "

"I *am* your friend, Davey. I'm so sorry. I didn't really mean what I said to Cara about you," Deena told him, feeling tears well up in her eyes.

Davey looked sad, too, but he didn't look as if he forgave her. "I think friends should stick up for each other," he said simply. "You can't just be a person's friend when it's convenient."

Had she really been doing that? Deena felt a sick shudder run through her as she realized that Davey was right. That was exactly what she'd done. But she had also truly come to value his friendship. And perhaps at that moment, as he was about to take his friendship away, she valued it more than ever.

"Davey—I know what I did was wrong. I can't tell you how sorry I am."

"O.K.—fine," Davey said with a shrug. "It's just that I don't think I want to see you anymore. Not for a while, anyway. I'd rather be by myself."

Deena bit her lip to stop herself from crying. He didn't forgive her. Why should he? She didn't deserve to be his friend after the way she had acted.

She stared at the ground, unable to meet his eyes. "If that's the way you feel, " she said in a small voice.

"Look, there are a lot of your things in the playhouse . . . your banjo and stuff."

"Oh, right . . . I'll come and get them sometime. Maybe tomorrow."

"All right. You can come any time. I have to go someplace at night, though," she added, remembering Cara's party.

"I'll come by at night, then," he said in a rush. "I'd rather."

"Oh—O.K.," Deena knew she was going to break down if she didn't get out of there fast. "Good-by, Davey," she said without looking at him. She turned and practically ran out the door.

Deena walked home under the stormy gray sky, her thoughts a confusing whirl. She had lost a friend. Davey didn't want to see her anymore. And she was so ashamed of the way she had talked about him in front of Cara. If only she had that moment to live over again, she would tell Cara what he was really like—and that she really liked being with him. Cara and her party didn't matter anymore. What mattered was that she didn't want to lose Davey's friendship, and now she didn't know if she would ever be able to get it back.

The rain began to fall—big, fat drops that soaked through her clothes and hair. Deena felt herself crying and wiped her hand across her eyes. Her tears were all mixed in with the raindrops. Now that she and Davey weren't friends anymore, the summer seemed as if it was going to be very long.

Chapter 10

Deena didn't tell anyone about what had happened with Davey. Not even Kathy. Kathy's band was going to play at Cara's party that night, and naturally Kathy was unbelievably excited. Saturday morning at the breakfast table she couldn't stop talking about it.

"Cara told me she was inviting about a hundred kids," Kathy told Deena in between bites of French toast. "It's going to be the greatest party. I sure hope it stops raining so we can set up the equipment outside," she rattled on. "I can't believe you helped us get this job, Deena. I mean, I thought you really hated Dementia."

"Cara asked me if you'd want to play, and I said I thought you would," Deena replied with a shrug. "That's all. I didn't really do anything that great."

"Well, whatever you said, it turned out to be great for us. She has good taste in music, you know," Kathy added in a serious tone. "For a cheerleader-type, I mean . . . You're going to the party, right?"

"Uh—oh, sure." Deena felt distracted, her thoughts wandering back to the sad scene in Davey's kitchen the night before.

"Deena? Do you feel all right?" her mother asked. Even if Kathy was too up to notice her cousin's mood, Deena's mother wasn't.

"I'm O.K. I don't feel great," she admitted, pushing her breakfast aside. "Maybe it's the rain."

"I hope you're not coming down with something," Lydia said in a worried tone. "Is Davey still sick? Maybe you caught something from him."

"Maybe," Deena said. She got up from the table, picked up her plate, and brought it to the sink. She was going to have to tell everyone that Davey had quit the play group and had quit being her friend. Sometime before Monday she also had to tell her mother and aunt why.

It was a rainy day, and the weather seemed to match Deena's mood perfectly. She played gin rummy with Mrs. Culver for most of the afternoon, then wrote a letter to her friend Pat and told her all about what had happened with Davey.

Pretty soon it was time to start getting ready for Cara's party. Kathy had to be there much earlier, to help set up the band equipment, and had left before Deena had even gotten in the shower.

"See you later, Deena," she had said brightly. "Wait till you hear us tonight. We're going to be great.

We're going to tear the place apart...I bet you can hardly wait to tell everyone at the party that you're related to me, right?"

"Be still, my fluttering heart!" Deena had said sarcastically, pressing her hand to her chest.

Kathy gave her a look. "Right...well, I won't tell anyone we're cousins, if you don't. O.K.?"

Once Kathy had left, Deena took a shower and washed her hair. She took her time getting dressed. She couldn't decide what she should wear. She didn't feel like going to a party, that was for sure, even if it was going to be the greatest trash night of the summer. Besides, Cara was about the last person she wanted to see.

When she was finally ready to leave, she said good-by to her mother and stepped out onto the front porch. She was surprised to see the weather had changed. The night was clear, with stars just beginning to appear in the darkening sky.

Cara lived only a short distance away and Deena planned to walk there. She started off down the front path, then realized she had never gotten together Davey's things in the playhouse. She had felt so bad, she had avoided going in there. But he was coming to pick them up tonight, so she forced herself to walk back to the shed.

There was still enough light outside for Deena to find her way around in the playhouse. She located Davey's banjo, a Frisbee, and a book on fossils. She put them all together on a table, then glanced around to see if she'd forgotten anything. On the windowsill something caught her eye. She couldn't believe it when she first saw it. The bottle that had held the cocoon now held a big orange and black butterfly.

Deena picked it up carefully and turned it over in her hands. The butterfly, moving its wings gently, seemed to be inspecting its branch. It was so delicate and beautiful, Deena felt as if she was holding something priceless. She knew that she should set it free, but then nobody else would see it. How long would the butterfly be able to stay alive inside the bottle? She didn't want it to die. Briefly, she thought about calling Davey to ask him; he would know what to do. Then she remembered that she couldn't call Davey. She decided to leave the bottle with the butterfly inside with his banjo and other belongings. She would write a note to him, too.

Deena found some paper and a pen and began writing the note. She tried a few times, but it kept coming out wrong. Finally she decided she wouldn't write a note at all; she would show him the butterfly herself.

She didn't have long to wait. A few minutes later she heard the sound of his bike.

"Hi, Davey," Deena said as he walked into the playhouse.

Davey stopped at the doorway. "Hi," he said stiffly. "What are you doing here? I thought you said you had to go someplace tonight."

"I did—Cara Bates is having a party."

He nodded. "Yeah, I know. I figured that's where you were going."

"I—uh—wanted to show you something," Deena

120

said, picking up the bottle. "Here, look at this . . . ." She stood up and handed the butterfly to him. "Isn't it something?"

"Wow!" Davey held the bottle up to the light. "It's gigantic. A monarch," he said, identifying its type.

It felt good to see him smiling again. Deena was glad now that she had waited for him instead of leaving a note. "I guess we have to let it go, right?"

"Yeah," Davey said, "it'll die in this bottle. Let's bring it outside."

They went outside with the bottle, and Davey carefully took out the twig that the butterfly clung to. Gently he put the twig down on the grass and stepped back. Deena didn't say a word as they watched the butterfly open it's wings and fly off into the night.

Neither of them spoke. Then Davey said, "Well, I guess I'd better get my stuff. You don't want to be late for Cara's party."

"Hey—wait. You don't have to go right away," Deena said. "I don't care if I'm late. I don't know if I really feel like going to that party after all," she admitted.

"You don't?" He stared at her, then pulled off his baseball cap and bounced it against his leg. "How come?"

"I don't know . . ." Deena shrugged. "I'm not in the mood for a big crowd, I guess. And all that Dementia noise," she added, rolling her eyes. "I was wondering if you maybe wanted to go into town and get some ice cream?"

Deena knew she had no right to act as if everything was all right between them, but something had just made her ask Davey the question. She felt her heart pounding furiously against the wall of her chest as she waited for his answer.

"Let me get this straight," Davey said slowly. "You want to go into town with me and have ice cream? Instead of going to Cara's party?"

"Uh-huh," she nodded.

"I don't understand," he said. He pulled on his baseball cap again. "I mean, I thought you were embarrassed for people to know that we were friends."

"I was—and I was wrong. It was terrible of me to act that way, Davey. It was really horrible," Deena admitted. "You were right to be angry. But I really want to try to be friends again. I promise I won't let you down ever again."

"Well—" Davey looked as if he wanted to believe her, but wasn't totally convinced. "The thing is, like I told you, I might move here to live with my dad . . . ."

"Really? That's great!" Deena said, and she really meant it.

"You think it's great?"

"Sure I do!"

"But, I mean, if we're friends again . . . you're not going to be embarrassed to hang out with me at school? I mean, when your boyfriend comes back?"

"We'll still be friends when Ken comes back," Deena promised. "Everything will be great. You'll like my friends, especially Pat. I wrote her all about you."

122

"You did?" Davey didn't seem to know what to say. "Well . . . gee . . . "

"Yeah, I did." Deena realized it was getting late. She didn't feel like going to Cara's party now. She didn't think much of Cara's friends, and she didn't really care what Cara thought of her. But she had a feeling that it would mean a lot to Davey if she invited him to go to the party. "So, you feel like going to a party with me?" Deena asked him.

Davey gave her a curious look—a mix of admiration and wariness. "Listen, Deena," he said, "I'm really glad you asked me to go with you. But I think I'll just skip it this time."

"Why? What's the matter?" Maybe he just feels nervous, Deena thought. Cara and her friends were pretty intimidating. "It'll be fine if you come with me," she assured him. "Cara won't care."

"I'm not worried about that," Davey said. "It's just that . . . well, I have to be honest. I really don't like that girl or her friends very much."

"Really?" Deena gave him a wide smile. "You know something? Neither do I," she admitted with a sigh of relief. "Feel like getting some ice cream instead?"

"Now there's a good idea," he said with a goofy smile. "Sure you don't have to wash your hair or anything?"

"Very funny, Findlay. I *was* going to buy you a banana split."

"A banana split? Hey, that reminds me of a joke . . . "

"You know, I had the strangest feeling it might," Deena said, smiling at him.

"Are you ready?" he asked, totally oblivious to her sarcasm. "This one is really funny," he said, tugging down on his cap.

"I'm ready," Deena said, bracing herself for another one of Davey's super corny jokes, and thinking how lucky she was to have found such a special friend.